ROYAL ELITE EPILOGUE

ROYAL ELITE BOOK 7

ROYAL ELITE
SCHOOL

RINA KENT

To the light after the dark.

AUTHOR NOTE

Hello reader friend,

Royal Elite Epilogue marks the end of Royal Elite Series. These books and these couples were such an experience, one I wouldn't forget for the rest of my life. I hope you enjoy their extended epilogue and the sneak peek into their future.

Please read to the very end. You don't won't to miss a few surprises.

To remain true to the characters, the vocabulary, grammar, and spelling of *Ruthless Empire* is written in British English.

Royal Elite Epilogue is set after the end of all the other books and cannot be read on its own. You have to read the previous books in the series first.

Royal Elite Series:
#0 Cruel King
#1 Deviant King
#2 Steel Princess
#3 Twisted Kingdom
#4 Black Knight
#5 Vicious Prince
#6 Ruthless Empire
#7 Royal Elite Epilogue

For more things Rina Kent, visit rinakent.com

ABOUT THIS BOOK

One final game.

All five couples of Royal Elite series come to
life again in this long extended epilogue.

Levi & Astrid.

Aiden & Elsa.

Xander & Kimberly.

Ronan & Teal.

Cole & Silver.

This epilogue is set after the end of Royal Elite Series
so all the previous books need to be read before this.

ROYAL ELITE EPILOGUE

ROYAL ELITE BOOK 7

PART ONE

The Proposal

ONE

Astrid

Age Twenty

"This isn't funny."

My heart almost beats out of my chest even as I try to keep my voice light-hearted.

The sound of the rain beats down all over the King's mansion, soaking the fountain in the middle of the back garden and the trees in the distance.

I should've known he was up to no good.

Levi is always up to no good.

"Levi?" I call in a hesitant voice as my steps falter near the covered hallway of the King's mansion.

I search around, expecting one of his distasteful pranks where he jumps me from behind.

I'll probably never admit this to him, but I love that part of him the most. There's never a dull moment with him.

He makes my days unforgettable and my nights as thrilling as a rollercoaster ride.

Yesterday, he saw me having lunch with a few of my college friends who somehow all ended up being males. Levi decided to be a dick and kiss me in front of all of them until I had to apologise and leave.

I'm still feeling sore from the way he took me hard and fast against the door as soon as we entered his flat.

It's his type of punishment. A game he plays with my body that I don't ever want to end.

As soon as we graduated, Levi chose to live on his own. He still didn't touch his trust fund and is living off his overflowing career with Arsenal. It amazes me how he can play and study at the same time. I feel so overwhelmed with the art classes alone.

On paper, I still live with Dad, but in reality, I crash in Levi's flat more often than not.

We practically live together now.

"Are you going to be petty for long?" I ask, rubbing my arms.

A chill covers my bare limbs and it's not because of the cold. A part of me is bubbling, itching and almost jumping out of my skin for what he plans to do.

Levi might have grown up, but he's still the same unpredictable arsehole who's out to flip my world upside down.

The only difference is that I love it. No, I crave it. Sometimes, I feel like his madness mirrors mine.

And when I wake up in the morning with this face next to mine, I say a silent prayer to always wake up next to him.

He might rock my world, but he's also the only one who's able to balance it. He's my anchor and my peace. He has some possessive and controlling issues, but that's part of who Levi King is.

In fact, after getting to know his uncle and his cousin, I can say Levi is the safest amongst them—shocker, I know.

They have something all screwed up in the family's blood.

They're all twisted in their own ways and they're unapologetic about it.

A sound catches behind me. I stop and glance sideways, my breathing hitching.

"Levi?"

Nothing.

I wait for a few long seconds and then release a breath. I'm going back inside. To hell with Levi's games.

Something crashes into me from behind. I shriek until I recognise his warmth and his unmistakable scent.

"What did I say about letting your guard down, Princess?" he speaks against my ear before he nibbles on the lobe. "That's when I'll always strike."

"You're awful." I try to control my heartbeat.

"You still love me for it."

"Maybe I don't anymore," I taunt. "Maybe I'm falling for someone else from my class."

"Do you really want the blood of all your classmates' on your hand?"

I gasp in mock reaction. "You wouldn't."

"Oh, I very much would."

Yup. He's crazy enough to do it.

Before I can say anything, he picks me up in his

arms. I gasp as he runs straight out to the rain, and I squeal with pure excitement as the water soaks us.

His lips slam into mine as he kisses me until I can only breathe him. It's desperate and robs my sanity and my entire surroundings.

He still consumes every inch of me with a single touch.

The feeling of being in the rain with him never gets boring. It's one of my favourite things to do with him.

Instead of spinning me around in his arms, he puts me down on my feet and steps back.

Before I can make out what's going on, he gets on his knees and fetches a ring with a huge diamond on top from his pocket.

"You gave my life meaning and I want to spend every single moment of it with you." He looks up at me with his wet blond hair sticking to his temples and his pale blue eyes shining with intensity. "Would you marry me, Princess?"

"Yes! A million times yes, Levi!"

I pull him to his feet and crush my lips to his as he slides the ring on my finger.

"I volunteer to be best man!" Ronan's voice shouts from behind us.

Levi and I stop kissing, but he's still holding me in the rain.

The four horsemen—Elites' current forward line—cheer with a lot of snark thrown in between.

In fact, only Dan, Xander, Ronan, and Cole cheer. Aiden leans against the wall with his ankles crossed and a bored expression written all over his face as he scrolls through his phone.

Last year, I thought Aiden could be mildly psychopathic, but now, I'm almost sure he has clinical antisocial disorder.

Nothing holds any value to him.

The only time I see him lose the bored expression is when he's around a certain Ice Princess.

"Oh, shit!" Dan exclaims with astonishment. "Does this make me the maid of honour?"

I laugh, the sound carefree and happy. "Sure does, Bug."

Dad walks out the front door, wearing a proud smile. Jonathan stands by his side, staring between his son and his nephew.

Sometimes, I think he wants Aiden to be more like Levi. At other times, it seems the exact opposite.

I wouldn't call Dad and Jonathan friends, but they tolerate each other enough to visit one another's homes when we invite them.

"I'm happy," I whisper to Levi. "Thank you for existing, my king."

He smiles. "Thank you for being mine, Princess."

And then he's kissing me again.

TWO

Aiden

Age Eighteen

Negative energy hums under the surface. It mounts and soars with every second. The loud music and drunk people at Astor's place aren't helping.

Knight passes me a joint, but I shake my head.

Fuck this shit.

I'm pissed off.

And I know exactly why I'm pissed off.

Tonight was a semi-final game and Elsa came to watch and stayed through the entire thing. Yes, she finally came to one of my games. This time, it was for me and not for some other fucker.

To top it off, she wore my T-shirt. Number eleven, King. I had to stop myself from flying off to the stairs, remove that shirt and fuck her on the spot.

All the annoying people present put a halt to my fantasy.

Instead, I gave it my all during the game. I might have scored two goals to see that spark in her blue eyes.

Unlike common belief, I'm a giver. I just take more than I give.

Now, back to tonight's actual problem. Elsa and I were supposed to go to the Meet Up where I could worship her body all night.

I had plans that started with her moaning and ended with her screaming my name.

See? A giver.

Last minute, Elsa decided she wants to come to Astor's fucking party. I told him to cancel it, but the twat disappeared somewhere to drink and fuck—probably at the same time.

I'm stuck here with a grumpy Knight who's been smoking more weed than a hippie and groaning like a divorced old man thinking about pensions.

Nash vanished. He's been disappearing without notice a lot lately.

Elsa is nowhere to be seen.

I pull out my phone and read our last conversation.

Elsa: Wait for me at Ronan's party.

Aiden: No.

Elsa: Come on. Do it for me?

Aiden: Still a no.

Elsa: Please?

Aiden: I'm fucking you all the way to Sunday at the Meet up. You don't get to change your mind.

Elsa: I didn't change my mind. You get to fuck me all the way to Sunday and more if you wait at Ronan's house.

That's the text that convinced me.

I shouldn't blame Nash for thinking with his dick when I do the same sometimes.

Okay, most of the time.

Elsa sent that text more than an hour ago, but she's still not here.

Van Doren is in the middle of the floor, dancing and flirting with all the girls he can see.

His goth sister is tucked in the corner, almost blending in with a plant. If the Marquis de Sade and Snow White had a spawn, it'd be her.

Usually, Elsa would be with them. If she's not, only one other person remains.

I nudge Knight with my elbow. "Where's Reed?"

"Fuck if I care."

"I didn't ask if you cared, I asked where she is." I hold up a hand. "And don't even pretend that you don't know where she is at all times."

He gives me one look over. "Even if I knew I wouldn't tell you. How about that, King?"

The little bitch.

I'm about to strangle the answer out of him when my phone vibrates.

Elsa: Remember our room in Ronan's place?

I don't even have to think about which room she's referring to. There's only one room in Astor's mansion that's completely ours.

"Hey, Knight?"

"What?" He grumbles from his seat next to me. He's been sitting there like a zombie for the past hour.

"Do you know what Reed said about you the other day?"

His eyes spark for the first time tonight. Sorry fuck.

He masks his reaction all too soon, though. "I don't care."

"Are you sure? It was kind of taboo."

His Adam's apple bobs with a swallow. When he speaks, his voice is quiet. "What did she say?"

"Even if I knew, I wouldn't tell you. How about that, Knight?"

I grin, walking away. I can feel him flipping me off even without having to turn around.

Taking the steps two at a time, I find myself on the second floor. The music from downstairs eventually fades.

My muscles tighten at the promise of finding Elsa. I haven't touched her since yesterday and something feels off.

I take back my thoughts about the possibility of getting enough of Elsa. It won't happen. Not in this lifetime.

My fucker friends tell me I'm too possessive. I ignore their comments in front of Elsa, but I mess with their lives any chance I get behind her back.

Since Elsa's been discharged from the hospital, she's become a new person.

For one, she's more open about her affection for me. She's more demanding when it comes to what she thinks is her right, but most of all, she's all in as much as I am.

I can now feel it when she opens her eyes and smiles instead of frowning. When she hugs me instead of pulling away.

We still live separately, but I plan to change that once we're at the university.

The fright she gave me at the hospital will never happen again. Dr Albert, her heart physician, has been watching her condition intently. The meds are enough to regulate her palpitations for now. She's stable and healthy, but he told us to keep a close watch on her in case she hides the worsening of her condition again.

Forget about her aunt, uncle, and father. I've become much worse than them when it comes to monitoring her. I can tell Elsa doesn't like it sometimes, but I made it clear that there will be no more fucking around with her health.

There's no way in fuck I'll let her be in danger like that time in the basement.

As soon as I arrive at the door, I push it open. The bedside lamp is the only light that's on.

This is where I first had Elsa all for myself and the first time she wrapped those lips around my cock.

My back leans against the door as I lock it. "Sweetheart?"

"In here," she calls from the bathroom. "One second."

"Take all the seconds," I call back as I remove my jacket, my shirt and then my trousers and boxer briefs.

If she thinks we're here to party, she has another thing coming.

I'm facing away from the bathroom, placing my clothes on the chair when tiny arms surround me from behind. Now I know how she can be so quiet when she moves. She gained that habit ten years ago when she snuck around to come meet me.

"Wow," she breathes against my back. "You're ready."

"I'm always ready, sweetheart."

Her lips find my back in a chaste kiss as she murmurs, "I'm also ready."

Her torso that's glued to my back is fully clothed so she can't be naked.

We can fix that.

I turn around and freeze.

Elsa stands in front of me with her hair falling on either side of her breasts. She's wearing my Elites' shirt with the number eleven and my last name on it.

She's obviously not wearing anything underneath judging by the visible peaks of her nipples. The thing barely covers her pussy. Her long, athletic legs are completely bare as she fidgets.

"What do you think?" she asks carefully. "Do you like it?"

"Like it?" I growl, lunging at her like a fucking caveman.

She squeals as I pick her up and throw her on the bed. Her arms loop around my neck and her legs wrap around my waist.

My lips find hers in a savage kiss, long and desperate.

I've been starving all day for her taste. "You know how much you made me wait, sweetheart?"

"Was it worth it?" she pants against my mouth, her chest rising and falling in a quick rhythm.

"Fuck right, it was, but you're going to make it up to me." I run my tongue over the shell of her ear. "I was promised to be able to fuck you all the way to Sunday."

She laughs, lust shining bright in her eyes. "And if I say no?"

"I'll fuck you all the way to Monday."

Challenge rises in her blue gaze. It's a game of ours, something we do when Elsa wants me to go rough and merciless on her.

"And if I say no again?" Her voice is barely a murmur.

"We can go on until Tuesday."

She reaches between us and runs her finger over my cock. It was semi-hard since she hugged me. At her touch, my dick snaps to life in an instant.

The fucking traitor is on an Elsa-Viagra pill. She's the only one who's able to revive him to life.

"Fuck, sweetheart. If you don't move your hand…"

"What?" she challenges.

"I'll tie you up," I whisper darkly into her ears and feel her sharp intake of air.

We don't do this often, but whenever we do, Elsa lets go completely. My little Frozen gets off on having her will taken away by me during sex. She's slowly admitting that fact to herself.

Baby steps.

She releases my cock and reaches to take off the T-shirt.

I clutch her hand, stopping her in her tracks. "I'm going to fuck you with my name branded on you, then you'll ride me wearing it. Then I'll take it off, tie your hands with it and fuck your little arse."

A red hue covers her cheeks. I revel in her reaction to my words as she nibbles on her bottom lip. "All the way to Sunday?"

"All the way to fucking Sunday, sweetheart."

My lips find hers as I ram inside her in one brutal go. My abs tighten with the ruthless force of my thrust. She arches off the bed. Her arms and legs grip around me like a vice.

In moments like these, when Elsa and I are one, the entire world vanishes.

The need to possess her beats under my skin and claws in my bones. It's more than an obsession or even an addiction. It's light in the darkness burning me from the inside out.

The more she holds on to me like I'm her anchor, the harder I fall into her warmth.

Being with Elsa is exactly like it was ten years ago. She always brought peace to my chaotic head.

The only difference is that I became more perverse about her company.

Kissing and hugging aren't enough anymore. Now, she's mine, body, heart and soul.

First, she engraved herself under my skin, then in my brain, and then into my heart. She made a cosy place for herself in there. Now, that damn thing only beats for her.

After I come deep inside her walls and bring her

to orgasm two times in a row, Elsa lies limp, appearing all spent.

I'll probably need to draw her a bath.

"Did I tell you how crazy your stamina is?" She rolls onto her side and props her elbow, facing me.

I tug on the T-shirt that's still covering her tits. "We still didn't do the round with this off."

"I give up." She laughs. "I completely give up."

"Good. Because I wasn't kidding. I keep my promises, sweetheart."

A twinkle shines in her bright eyes as she nibbles on her bottom lip. She then releases it fast, thinking I won't be able to read that gesture.

It's useless. I already know she has something in that busy head of hers.

"What is it?"

She says nothing.

My lips tug in a smirk. "Tell me or I'll add another round of thorough fucking."

"You said you keep all your promises," she starts.

"I do."

"How about promises from ten years ago?"

So it's about that. I smile on the inside, but I show her nothing. "I don't know. You still didn't decide on your university."

We've been talking about this for the past few months. I was more than willing to ditch Oxford and go to Cambridge—even if it's not the best for business management and it'd piss Jonathan off.

None of that mattered. I already decided Elsa and

I will live together at university. I won't do the whole long-distance bullshit.

"I'm ditching Oxford," I tell her matter-of-factly. I don't care what anyone has to say about it.

"Bummer." She pouts. "I was thinking of applying there."

"You were?"

"Yes. Dad and I talked and I decided to go back to my initial dream."

"Your initial dream?"

"Yeah. I showed you the drawings when I was young."

"Building houses."

She nods frantically. "I'll go to the School of Architecture at Oxford."

"And we'll live together." I know I'm burning steps, but I have to hit the iron while it's hot.

Truth is, I can never get enough of Elsa. It kills me to send her back home every other night.

I want her with me all the fucking time. I want to sleep surrounded by her warmth every night and wake up to her face every morning.

I expect her to fight and tell me she needs to think about it.

My mind is already filled with a thousand ways to convince her. I can sabotage her dorm application. I can trick her into thinking she's rented a house with a roommate and then surprise her by showing up. I can—

Elsa reaches under the bed and brings out a bucket of chocolates. She kneels by my side, cradling the thing as her face turns bright red.

A bucket of chocolate? What the fuck?

Wait.

The name of the brand stares back at me.

Maltesers.

"When I grow up, I'm gonna buy you a bucket of Maltesers."

"Why?"

"Because Dad says you have to buy gifts for the one you marry."

"Marry?" I whisper.

"Yup!" She grins. "When I grow up, I'm going to marry you."

"I'm keeping my promise, too," she murmurs.

"You're not the one proposing, I am." I groan, pulling her and the stupid bucket into me. "I'm going to fucking marry you, Elsa. You'll be my wife. My family. My fucking home."

She nods several times, tears shining in her eyes. "You'll be my home, too, Aiden. Always."

Always.

I crash my mouth to hers.

Elsa is mine.

Fucking mine.

Just like I'm hers.

Always.

Next up, I'm going to put a fucking baby in her.

THREE

Kimberley

Age Twenty-One

I wake up submerged in pleasure.

Literally.

My legs are wide open as Xander feasts on my pussy. His wicked tongue runs up, then thrusts inside me.

I back off the bed and grab his blond strands with a force that must hurt. That doesn't stop him, though.

He eats me like a hungry predator and I'm his poor, willing prey.

His thumb finds my clit and he does that masterful thing, flicking and circling. It's insane how much better he knows my body than I do. How he drives me crazy with the simplest touches.

The moment he teases it between his fingers, I'm a goner.

Complete and utter goner.

I scream his name as I come undone around his tongue. My breathing is harsh and fast as he licks my sensitive folds one more time.

When his face reappears from between my legs, he's grinning so wide that his dimples form deep creases in his cheeks.

He darts his tongue out and licks me off his lips, and I can't help the whimper that escapes me.

Oh, God.

That will never get old.

Since we started living together when we started college three years ago, Xander always wakes me up this way or with his dick deep inside me. Bottom line, he always wakes me up with an orgasm and those mischievous dimples.

I try to wake him with my lips around his cock, but that doesn't happen too often. One, he's always up first, and two, he usually doesn't like it when I take away his 'morning fun' as he calls it.

"Morning, beautiful." He climbs my body with slow, sloppy kisses up my belly.

I stopped my life-draining diet two years ago. It took too much to make that decision, so as soon as I began to keep my food in, I decided to adopt a healthy lifestyle but without starving myself.

Xander became my personal trainer for runs, and I might have wanted to kill him at the beginning for all the long jogs we did, but then I started to look forward to them. And, okay, the way he looked in his running clothes might have helped a bit. Fine, a *lot*.

He's just delicious, and all the girls who jog in our park agree.

When I glared at them, he teased me and told me while fucking me that I'm the only woman he sees and ever will.

True, I still have those self-confidence issues sometimes, but now, I have my mechanisms and I've learnt how to easily move away from them by digging into my self-empowerment.

Now, I can look at myself in the mirror and finally smile. I can be myself and not want to be someone else.

And the person who played the most important role in all of that is this man who's now kissing his way up my body—my non-perfect, full of stretch marks and scars body—and still has that wild, lustful look in his eyes.

He flicks my nipple with the pad of his thumb and I moan deep in my throat and run my fingertips over the place where his heart lies. He had a tattoo inked on his skin as soon as he returned from rehab and stayed away from Absolut Vodka. We do drink, but he never loses himself to it now.

Green.

That's what's on the tattoo. Just one word next to his heart.

He got me inked on him for life, and I still feel close to tears whenever I see it.

Xander is mine as much as I'm his.

His chest sticks to mine as he grins at me with that sloppy, sleepy, lustful smile.

"Morning, Xan." I ruffle his blond hair. I can't keep my hands off it and I might be too in love with the colour. It's shining under the morning light coming from the balcony of our bedroom.

He leans on his elbows so they're on either side of me. "Happy graduation."

"Ugh, don't remind me of all the things I have to do today. Kir was demanding to come here."

Dad, Lewis, and Kirian will join us for lunch after the graduation ceremony, and then I've already made plans with Elsa, Aiden, and the others.

That is, if Aiden doesn't decide to kidnap Elsa somewhere.

We always have family lunches and dinners now. Lewis and Dad are our fathers, and although I don't call Lewis 'Dad' and Xan doesn't do the same to my dad, we have that unspoken mutual understanding, sort of like the one Dad and Lewis had for years.

It's easier this way and doesn't give us grief from any prying eyes.

Mum moved to Paris two years ago. She sends us invitations to her exhibitions, but we don't go. There isn't even any pain as we talk about her now. She's like that distant relative no one actually cares about.

Even Kirian, who's supposed to be attached to his mother, doesn't want to spend time with her and is now striving to be a 'proper' man like Dad and his Uncle Lewis—his words, not mine.

"I'll bribe Kirian with brownies so he doesn't spend the night," Xander says.

"Why can't he?"

"Because we're celebrating."

"We'll be doing a lot of celebrations for one night."

"We'll have to add one more then. The most important one." He reaches under the pillow and retrieves a ring with a blinding green jewel on top.

My eyes widen as I stare between him and the ring. This can't be what I think it is...?

"I've wanted to do this since RES, but Dad and Calvin said all that adult shit about college graduation and whatnot. Besides, I didn't want to distract you more than I should. Needless to say, I've waited so fucking long to make you officially mine, to call you my wife, my life, and my future."

I'm crying like a little girl by the time he finishes. "Yes! Absolutely yes!"

"I wasn't asking. That means you have the chance to say no and I'm not having that, Green." He slips the ring on my finger. Perfect fit—of course it is.

Sometimes, I think Xander knows me even better than I know myself.

He stops and looks at me more than I'll ever stop to look at myself.

And for that reason, he's not only perfect for me, but he was made for me.

Just like I was made for him.

"I love you so much, Xan."

"And I love you, Green." He claims my mouth in a slow kiss that robs my breath.

I'm melting and I have no interest in stopping it.

London, our cat, mewls, then jumps on the bed, demanding to join the celebration. She hates being left out.

Xander pulls away, "Now, for the wedding date."

"What about it?"

"How about tomorrow?"

We both laugh as our lips meet again.

FOUR

Teal

Age Nineteen

There's something about seeing the world through different lenses.

Before, it was blurry. Now, there's sense to it, a clarity I wasn't able to feel before.

There's something called happiness, and there's something called joy.

For my whole life, I never actually understood what happiness meant and why people would crave to be happy. It felt like a high that would just eventually wear off.

That is, until Ronan became a constant in my life. He's happiness incarnate.

He's a high that will never wear off.

After we graduated, we spent the summer

travelling. Just that, travelling, from one country to another and from one city to the next.

We were free souls discovering the world and people and cultures. He called me a nerd whenever I asked about museums, and I called him a gigolo whenever he wanted to go to the trendiest bar.

Ronan will be Ronan no matter what happens. Fun and parties are in his soul. Whenever anyone needs a party thrown, he'll be at the front of the line planning his next 'epic' event. The last was Aiden and Elsa's marriage. He was so extra in his speech, acting salty because he wasn't the best man.

Since then, he's been bribing Xander to be chosen as the best man, threatening to delete them all from his group chat.

He won't.

What he doesn't tell them is that the horsemen saved him from his head several times in the past. They weren't there just for the parties, like most other people; they were there for him, and Ronan would never forget that.

To say we're both over Eduard would be a lie. Sometimes, it feels as if he's still the shadow looming over our lives, even after his death.

Ronan and I still have the nightmares, but they're sparse and far between. We go to joint therapy now, and it's the best therapy I've had in my life.

When it gets to be too much, I just say it. However, it usually doesn't, because I know I have my family, and most of all, I have *him*.

Ronan.

The moment he strokes my hair off my face or kisses me, I usually climb his body and demand that he fucks me.

Of course, he obliges, and he makes it dreamier every time, rougher, harder. Ronan has never treated me as if I'm a delicate flower, and I love him the most for it. Even when he fucks me slow, it's to make me feel him—feel us—not because he's afraid of touching me.

Ronan and I are never afraid of touching each other. If anything, it's what brings us closer and makes us calmer.

We started with a touch. The first time he did it in RES's library, I kind of fell under his spell and he fell under mine.

Today, I have a surprise for him.

We came to his parents' house for dinner. Charlotte is finally out of the danger zone. Those couple of months after Eduard's death were complete hell.

Edric had to make his brother's death seem like an accident, and Charlotte's illness was taking its toll on him and Ronan. I held my fiancé's hand through it all until the results came out and the doctor said the last surgery had been a success.

She had to do a lot of recovery therapy, and Edric didn't leave her side through it all. Ronan didn't either.

One of my favourite memories about that time was when Edric asked Ronan for forgiveness for not seeing Eduard's actions, and Ronan said he was sorry he hadn't seen his mum's illness.

Edric and Ronan grew so close during Charlotte's recovery journey. I think seeing them together by her side helped her mental state more than any doctor would tell them.

Ronan and I were supposed to leave after dinner, but he said he needed to grab something from his room.

He's been taking a long time, so I might as well ask him now.

"Lars." I grin when I see him coming out of Ronan's room. "How do I look?"

I pull on my white T-shirt, on which is written 'Belle'.

I'm also wearing a black tulle skirt, a leather jacket, and boots—comfy, as usual.

"That's the second time you've asked me that question tonight, Miss Teal."

"Stop being such a snob, and it's only Teal," I tease.

Lars and I have grown close over time. He wouldn't admit it, but he always has a dark chocolate bar ready for me then he whines about how I keep stealing them.

"You look beautiful." He lifts his chin. "And stop eating the chocolate no one offers you."

I make a face as he strides down the hall then I go into the room.

Okay, this is it.

It's not like it needs to be traditional or something—not that I care about that anyway.

"Hey, Ronan, when are we getting married…?"

I trail off when I find him in the middle of removing his trousers in front of a bed filled with baskets of dark chocolate.

"Fuck, *belle*, you weren't supposed to come in yet."

I grin. "Don't stop on my account."

His hands remain on his belt. "Lars said dark chocolate is the best bribe I could use with you."

"Lars wasn't wrong."

"Wait." His hand leaves his belt, and I nearly reach over to put it back.

Ronan is so beautiful, sometimes I stay up just to stare at him.

It's not only his physical beauty, though; it's also his soul that speaks to me and wrenches me out of my own soul.

He's the calm after the storm.

He's the light after the darkness.

He's everything.

"Go back." He narrows his eyes. "Did I hear something about marriage?"

"Yeah. I thought…you know…we'd make things official?" Otherwise I'll start punching every girl who looks at him at uni.

He still attracts attention like a magnet. I thought that would be over after RES, but nope, his popularity knows no limits. I need to stake my claim before anyone tries to take him away.

It's not that I'm threatened or anything, but I'm as greedy about Ronan as he is about me. That will probably never change.

People say we're too young to get married, but it's not about age for me. I've decided Ronan is the only human being I'll spend the rest of my life with. It's a cemented fact. So why delay it?

"Hey." He appears offended. "I was planning a night out to ask you. This is not fair."

"You wanted to ask me?"

"I wanted to marry you before that fucker Aiden married Elsa, but you always say all the grandiose stuff is stupid, so I figured I'd wait."

My heart skips a beat as I stand on my tiptoes, wrap my arms around his neck, and seal a kiss to his cheek. "It isn't stupid when you're involved, Ronan."

His grin widens. "One-nil, Xander."

I laugh. "So does this mean you'll marry me?"

"Of course I'm marrying you, and you didn't ask first—I did."

"We'll agree to disagree, your lordship," I tease. "What did you have in mind with the chocolate?"

"A few things." His eyes shine with mischief.

"Like what?"

"Like this." His lips meet mine, and then we're falling on the bed.

If this is my life going forward, I'm so ready for it.

FIVE

Silver

Age Twenty-One

"What the hell are you doing here?" I whisper-yell as Cole leans against the bathroom's door and clicks it closed behind him. "This is the ladies' room."

"I know." He stalks towards me, and every step he takes is like he's walking straight to my heart.

I was right. There's no way my feelings for him would ever fizzle out.

With every passing day, I fall harder and faster into him.

With every day, he becomes my everything.

We moved to Oxford for university, and soon after, we told Mum and Papa about our relationship.

I can't be with him officially. At least, not yet. Papa

won the election and became the prime minister, then remarried Mum a year after Helen's death.

That caused quite a ruckus in the media, despite their strategic approach. Frederic made it look like Mum consoled Papa and they rediscovered their initial attraction.

It's true that Cole and I don't live under the same roof anymore, and he eclipsed himself from the family circle to not be associated as my brother. But it'll take years for the world to come to terms with us.

We're bigger than the world, he and I. They're not ready for us.

Papa and Mum are the Conservative Party—despite their non-conservative actions with that affair. I can't exactly bring their votes down by announcing I'm in love with my ex-stepbrother.

I can only do that once Papa is out of 10 Downing Street.

Because of that, our relationship is just known on a familial and close friends level. As in only Aiden, Xander, and Ronan from our friends.

But even with that, Cole shouldn't be here.

"Everyone else is outside," I scold. "We're supposed to be celebrating Xander and Kim's engagement."

"I know." His eyes gleam as he cages me against the counter, his hands on either side of me.

I wrap both arms around his neck. "We can't do this."

"I know."

And then his lips devour mine. I climb up his body

as he fiddles with his belt, and soon enough he's plunging inside me.

I kiss him like a madwoman as he fucks me hard, fast and dirty against the counter of the bathroom.

I'd be lying if I said this was our first time violating public indecency codes. Cole doesn't show it, but he's the adventurous type. He doesn't stop when he wants something done—that something being me.

Nothing deters him, whether we're at the university dorms or during a night out while everyone is getting drunk. And even during family dinners.

Mum calls him out on it every time, and he merely shrugs.

"C-Cole…" I grip his shoulders hard.

"Close, Butterfly?" he grunts against my mouth.

"Yes, oh, yes."

"Who do you belong to?"

"You."

"Say it."

I bite my lower lip as I murmur the words that drive him crazy, "I've only loved you. Just you. You're my first and last."

He wraps his hand around my throat, squeezing as he pounds into me faster, making me fall.

Fall into him.

Fall into us.

He comes inside me at the same time as I shatter around him, biting his shoulder over his shirt to muffle my scream.

Once the wave subsides, I sigh, resting my head

against the crook of his neck, breathing him in. "I love you."

Instead of all the times I told him I hate him after sex, now I make it a habit to say my true feelings.

"And I love you." He kisses my nose as I stand to my unsteady feet, stupid gravity pulling me down.

After I clean him and myself up, I face the sink to check my makeup. Cole remains at my back, wrapping both arms around my middle.

Not a day goes by where we don't keep our hands off each other. We might not touch in public, but in private? We're everything no one should know.

We're kinky, we're dorks, we're nerds. Or, rather, Cole is. We're in love. We're happy.

As long as I have him, I know I won't need anything else.

He rests his chin on the top of my head. "You'll marry me, right?"

I freeze, the lipstick suspended in front of my parted mouth as I meet his gaze in the mirror. "W-What?"

"You'll marry me?"

"Is this because everyone else is getting married?"

"Fuck everyone else. I'm asking *you*." He kisses the top of my head. "I know it'll be a long time until I actually marry you, but I want confirmation."

"Oh, Cole." I spin around and face him. "Of course, I'll marry you. You're the only one for me."

"The only one, huh?"

"The *only* one."

"And you're the only one for me, Butterfly." He

kisses me so passionately on the lips, I nearly climb his body all over again.

"Repeat that in front of that fucker Aiden when we go outside."

I laugh. Cole is still low-key mad at Aiden for the three years I was engaged to him, and he seizes every chance to take revenge.

Cole will always be Cole.

I'm just glad he finally put Helen behind him. We both did. Now, we only focus on us.

When he demanded my firsts, I saved them for him. In return, he saved me his. We're each other's everything.

Hugging him, I whisper, "One day, I'll shout at the top of the world that you're mine."

"And you're mine, Silver, always."

"Always."

PART TWO

The Marriage

SIX

Levi

Age Twenty

If someone had told me a few years ago that I would be standing here today, I wouldn't have believed them.

Me, standing in the aisle when I'm barely twenty?

Me, waiting for the most beautiful woman on earth to come and complete my life?

The first day I met Astrid in Uncle's holiday mansion, when she was drugged and acted clingy, I wouldn't have thought we would end up here. I didn't realise how meaningless my life had been up to that point.

Completely, utterly meaningless.

As per Jonathan and Lord Clifford's demands, the hall in which our wedding is taking place is huge. They didn't want their offspring's wedding to be small and cosy, because they care a lot about image and all that rubbish.

If it were up to me, I would've kidnapped her to Jonathan's island and had a wedding only for the two of us.

However, I know how much she needs her friends with her and how much she's been preparing for this over the last couple of months. Astrid's parents got married in Vegas and never actually had a wedding, so she wanted a real one as a sort of gesture to her mother.

So here I am, standing while everyone is seated in neat rows with golden ornaments. I don't focus on the grandiose of the hall or the big names who've shown up for Uncle's and Lord Clifford's sakes.

I couldn't even if I wanted to.

My impatience is getting the best of me, and with each passing second, I regret not taking Astrid's hand and eloping about a year ago.

Everyone says we're too young to get married, but everyone wasn't slammed with the connection Astrid and I have had since the very beginning. The type of relationship we have isn't only healing, but it's also peaceful. When the outside world gets too loud, it's Astrid's embrace that silences it. When my head gets dark, it's Astrid's voice that soothes it.

Sometimes, I feel like I'm sucking on her life essence, yet whenever she crawls into my embrace as if she's always belonged there and tells me about her day, I feel like the luckiest bastard alive.

Yes, I'm selfish about that woman, and I have no plans to let her go. But I do plan to make her the queen of my life, the soul of my being, and the heart of my existence.

"Do you have the rings?" I whisper to Aiden, who's standing by my side.

I had no choice but to have the little shit as my best

man. Though Ronan or even Daniel would've been better, Aiden said he wants to.

Like he *really* wants to.

And I have no doubt that it's because Elsa is sitting somewhere in the crowd. She became close with Astrid during the past few months, and they even share girls' time now.

Aiden has a thing about wanting to be the centre of Elsa's attention, even if he's only the best man.

Not that I'm any different. In fact, I'm more obvious about it. I don't like sharing Astrid's time with anyone.

Her father and her best friend, Daniel, are already too much. I don't need to add names to the list.

"I think I forgot them." Aiden's poker face remains the same.

"What?" I hiss and catch Jonathan's glare in my peripheral vision.

He likes me and Aiden to be on our best behaviour in public to not sully the King name and blah fucking blah. Usually, my cousin and I abide by that rule to avoid his wrath.

But usually isn't today, because I'm seconds away from punching my cousin in the throat.

"You had one mission, Aiden!" I whisper-yell. "One fucking mission."

He pats his jacket and retrieves a small black velvet box. "Oh, looks like they're here, after all."

I narrow my eyes on him. "Did you do that on purpose?"

He lifts a shoulder. "You were being fidgety. I got your mind off things."

"Fuck you."

"You're welcome, Lev."

Astrid's bridesmaid walks down the aisle, carrying a bouquet of red roses. Murmurs filter through the attendees at the unconventional choice of a bridesmaid, but did they really expect my free-spirited Astrid to do everything according to tradition?

Daniel grins, bowing and winking at the audience. The old ladies break out in smiles as he gives each of them a flower. By the time he gets to the front, he has none left, except for the one attached to his tuxedo's pocket.

He stands opposite me and Aiden, and I resist the urge to ask him how she looks and if she's coming right this second.

"She's stunning," Daniel whispers to me as if hearing my unspoken question. "I don't think you're ready for her, Captain."

"I'm always ready for her," I mutter back.

Daniel gives me his cocky smirk, and while he's usually pasted to Astrid with superglue, I haven't ever felt threatened by him. They have a special bond that's never gone beyond friendship. The fact that he agreed to be the maid of honour for her sake says something about how far they're both willing to go for each other.

It's sort of like me and Aiden, but in my and my cousin's case, we've only ever bonded through our rivalry and the innate need to prove ourselves to Uncle Jonathan.

Astrid and Daniel are the pure form of us. Their relationship is more about lifting each other up instead of bringing the other down.

Even though Daniel chose an entirely different field of study than Astrid and they don't share the same passions—he prefers physical activities and partying while she's an introvert artist—they still find time for each other.

Of course, that time needs to be reduced once she becomes my wife. I might approve of Daniel, but I need her attention on me at all times.

Obsessive? Probably. After all, she's always been my obsession.

The music changes to an acoustic version of one of Muse's songs and I smile. Only Astrid would make her favourite band's song her wedding song.

I love that woman more than words can describe.

And Daniel was right. I'm not ready.

The moment she shows up, her hand tucked into Lord Clifford's arm, I stop breathing for a second.

She's…breathtaking.

Her white tulle dress falls to below her knees in a weirdly beautiful way. And she's wearing her signature fishnet stockings and sneakers instead of heels.

I tried to sneak a peek at her dress before the wedding, but she and Daniel shooed me away. Never in my wildest dreams did I think she'd be this breathtaking. Though to say I'm surprised she picked something like this would be a lie. Astrid has always been the type who owns up to her quirks without caring about societal standards.

The fact that she's so real is what made me fall for her this deeply and why I could never find a way out.

Not that I'd ever want to.

A huge grin lights up her features as her intense green eyes meet mine. She's more than ready to belong to me. Just like I can't wait to belong to her, now and beyond.

Lord Clifford places his daughter's hand in mine and says low, so only I can hear him, "I'm giving you a piece of myself and if you hurt her in any way, I will murder you. Not even Jonathan will be able to save you."

"Dad!" Astrid whisper-yells at her father, but she can't wipe the grin off her face.

I give a curt nod, and he brushes his lips against his daughter's forehead. "Be happy. You deserve it, Star."

Then he joins a solemn-faced Uncle, who hates everyone and everything in this world—especially Lord Clifford. Let's hope they don't burn the place down before the ceremony ends.

"Lev?" Astrid's eyes meet mine, and I take my time committing this face to memory.

It's almost like I'm seeing her for the first time.

This moment is too special to just let it go without engraving it in the box inside my heart that has her name all over it.

Her dark brown hair is pulled up, revealing her delicate throat that's surrounded by a star necklace I gave her as an early wedding gift. Her makeup is barely there, as usual, but she couldn't look any prettier than she does right now.

If there was a way to screenshot this moment and safekeep it, I wouldn't hesitate.

"Levi," she calls again. "The priest is talking."

"He has to wait until I get my fill of you."

Her cheeks redden as she smiles.

"You're blushing, Princess. I love it when you blush."

She tightens her clutch around my fingers and I vow to myself in this moment that from today onwards, this woman will be the reason I'm alive.

SEVEN

Aiden

Age Nineteen

Whoever invented the thing about not being allowed to see your bride before the wedding is a fucking idiot. If I could find him somewhere, he'd be finished.

But hey. Not seeing Elsa beforehand means there will be a surprise element, and I'm here for that. *Mostly*.

"Can't you get one thing fucking straight?" I glare at the bowtie in the mirror and then at the fucker sitting behind me who's reading from a book as if this were an everyday occurrence. "Choosing you as the best man is the worst decision I've ever made."

Cole turns a page. At least he looks presentable in his tux with the neat bowtie and the elegant shoes. "No one said anything about fixing ties. Besides, you didn't choose me. You're stuck with me, King."

"I did choose you." I completely remove the bow-tie and start from scratch.

"If I remember correctly, Xan said he'd have Ronan as his best man, and Ronan said he'd reciprocate because he doesn't like us most days and wouldn't allow either of us to ruin his wedding day. So you, being an arsehole, wouldn't have picked either of them, knowing they wouldn't reciprocate. Since your cousin hurt his leg, he wouldn't be able to stand for a long time. That makes you stuck with me. You're welcome, by the way."

"Fuck you, Nash." I yank off the bowtie again because it's still wrong. "You'll be stuck with me in your wedding, too. You better be prepared for what I'll do then."

"I'm more than prepared. After all, all this is happening for a purpose." Nash tilts his book to the side to watch me through the mirror. "Wait a second. Are you nervous?"

"Piss off."

A Cheshire cat grin appears on his lips as he abandons his book on the red velvet chair and stands up to join me by the mirror, watching me intently as if he's a cat who found a fish. "You are, aren't you?"

"Are you going to be useful anytime soon?"

His grin widens. "Not until you admit you're nervous. Aww, should I have been a good best man and got you a hooker last night?"

"If you had done that, I'd be getting Queens a male stripper on her wedding night." I grin back, and his falls as he flips me off.

He heads back to the chair. "Looks like you don't need help, after all. You can have a wedding without the bowtie."

"Nash…" I warn.

He stops midway and throws me a glance over his shoulder. "Do you admit it?"

"I'm *not* nervous."

"Yeah, right."

"I'm not. I'm just…" I release a long breath. "I can't believe this is happening. My mind keeps sending these signals that something will go wrong, like back when we were eight or afterwards, when she didn't remember me."

"Or maybe she'll one day wake up and realise she deserves better than you."

"You fucking—" I'm about to punch him in the face but stop myself because I can't have my best man with a bloodied nose.

"Relax." He smiles a little. "I was speaking from my point of view. That's what I think Silver will do every day. It's not a fun feeling."

I exhale deeply. "At all."

We remain in awkward silence for a few seconds. Neither Cole nor I are good with directing feelings to the outside. We're inward people and I think that's why we gravitated towards each other in the first place.

He takes the bowtie from my fingers and straps it around my throat, aiming his attention on it. "Elsa chose you when she could've gone with someone different."

"If you don't stop saying shit like that, you're going to get punched, and fuck having no best man."

He chuckles. "Just saying. My point is, she chose you and she knows exactly what she's in for. If she still hasn't given up on you yet, I say it's for the long haul."

"Long haul?"

"As long as you make it, King."

He finishes off and steps back to stare at his handiwork. "There. Done."

The door flies open and in comes Ronan, holding Xander's shoulder as they laugh about something while stuffing their faces with appetisers.

As soon as they see us, Ronan barges between me and Nash, holding an imaginary microphone. "Yo, King. How does it feel to be getting married?"

"Nervous." Nash smirks and I flip him off while smoothing my jacket.

"I've got to admit, I thought I would be the first one to get married." Xander pouts. "But I guess my father is stricter than Jonathan King."

"Jonathan is strict." Cole retrieves his book. "Aiden just doesn't give a fuck."

"Okay, Aiden wins in the wedding department." Astor points a finger at himself. "But my Teal and I got engaged first. We'll get married before you know it, so try to beat us, Xan."

"Oh, you're on." Xander hits his shoulder playfully and the latter returns it.

They start one of their bickering sessions before I turn around and ask, "Have you seen Elsa?"

"Fuck yeah. She was my fiancée first, remember?"

"And my girlfriend." Xan grins.

I'm about to jam their faces into the wall when they burst out laughing and mocking me while Nash smirks in the background like the little bitch he is.

The door opens again before I can ask them how she looks. Not that I should. I want to see how she is for myself.

Levi hobbles in, leaning on his crutch. He had a small injury during a game, but he needs to rest for a bit before he can resume practice. Despite the crutch, he appears his best in a tux and with his blond hair styled.

"Looking good, little Cousin." He approaches me and squeezes my shoulder in a hug, then releases me. "Ready to join the marriage train?"

Not really. This isn't about marriage for me. It's about being with Elsa for as long as possible. It's about the life we'll have together and the memories we'll make in the future. It's about becoming one.

Am I ready for that?

I smile in the mirror.

Abso-fucking-lutely.

Half an hour later, I'm standing in front of the aisle in Ethan's house. That's where Elsa wanted the wedding, and Jonathan wasn't the least bit pleased about it, but he'll live. This day isn't about him, it's about her.

Cole is on his best behaviour at my right, which has to do with the girl who's sitting a few rows across from us with her parents. Silver smiles at him but quickly averts her gaze because they're still at the stage where their relationship is a secret.

Teal is hanging on to Ronan's arm as he whispers things in her ear, then grins like an idiot. Xan is sitting with Knox in the front row and sulking like an abandoned kid because Kimberly is standing opposite me as the maid of honour.

I'm focused on anyone but myself because my impatience is getting the better of me.

Just when I'm about to send Cole to look for Elsa, the music changes. I straighten as Ethan appears with the most beautiful creature I've ever seen.

It's like a recurrence of those times when she first found me in that basement—when her eyes met mine, and she told me she'd save me.

She did in more ways than one.

Now, she's doing it again.

Her full white dress outlines her soft curves and its hem sweeps the floor. She didn't pull up her hair like I expected her to. Instead, the blonde strands are intertwined with flowers as they fall to the sides of her face. She has no veil, and her expression is bright, soft, and so alive, I want to run there and place my ear to her chest in order to listen to her heartbeat.

When her electric blue eyes meet mine, the world stops moving for a second.

It's only the two of us, like when we were eight and she told me she'd marry me. When she made me promise her the same.

We're both making that promise a reality, and

because of that, today is another beginning of our lives together.

Elsa's lips pull in a smile and I smile back.

She's always been mine, when we were eight and when I reunited with her again at sixteen and when I finally got her at eighteen.

I was lucky to find her and I'll spend the rest of my life making her feel like the queen she has always been.

Now and forever.

EIGHT

Xander

Age Twenty-One

When Kim said she wanted to get married in this place, I thought she was joking.

But I should've known better. There's no joking about such things with my Green.

I adjust the cuffs of my jacket as I wait for her to appear at the end of the aisle.

The wedding planner turned the small park where we used to play as kids into a piece cut from heaven. Lights fall over the trees and form a path on either side of where the attendees are sitting.

It's cosy and small, and we only invited the people who actually mean a fuck to either of us. Needless to say, neither my mother nor Kim's mother were invited.

Jeanine sent a congratulations card that Kim barely

looked at before she pushed it to the middle of the endless wedding gifts we received.

We don't need the toxicity of our mothers' in our lives. Those women were never meant to give birth to children in the first place, and while I could get over that fact with time, Kim is different. She loves too deep and doesn't hold grudges. Evidence? She forgave me when I shouldn't have been forgiven.

She also forgave Silver, who's currently standing with Elsa opposite Ronan and me. Not only has she picked up her friendship with Silver, but it's like the years in between never existed. It took them some awkward moments during university, but they soon returned to being the two girls who barged in on Aiden, Cole, and me when we were young and demanded to play with us.

The Silver and Kim from those times were so tight and inseparable that I hated Silver sometimes.

What? Kim wasn't the only one who was possessive about the other's time. I didn't like that she shared a connection with any other person. I still don't, but I'm better at compromising right now—I think.

"Stop it!" Ronan whisper-yells in my ear. "You're making me look like a loser best man with your fidgeting, *connard*."

"Shut the fuck up, Ron. You're already married."

"That I am." He winks at Teal, who's standing beside Silver, and she shakes her head with a smile. It escapes me how she keeps up with this disaster of a man on a daily basis.

"You're not supposed to be noisy at weddings," Cole says from his position beside Ronan.

"You're not supposed to be here in the first place, Cole," I grumble, then shoot a glare at Aiden. "You either, King."

"Nonsense," he says. "If Elsa is here, I have the right to be here, too."

"Besides." Cole pokes Ronan. "If you only had Ronan, your wedding would be destined to fail before it even starts."

"Hey—" Ronan opens his mouth, probably to curse him, but he stops mid-sentence when Kim appears, one hand laced through Calvin's arm and the other through Kirian's.

While both are wearing tuxedos, Kirian's is white, like the colour of his sister's dress. He's just twelve, but he's grown so much now, and he insisted that he'd be giving away Kim, too, because he's her brother and protector.

That little guy isn't so little anymore.

It takes me a few seconds to completely take Kimberly in. The way her brown hair with green highlights falls to her shoulders. The way her white dress has a green ribbon at the middle to match the bright colour of her eyes.

When her gaze meets mine, she bites her lower lip slightly before releasing it.

Fuck me.

That woman will be the death of me. It didn't happen when we were kids, but it sure as fuck is going to now.

I wait for her to reach my side, then Calvin puts her hand in mine. My biological father and I exchange a look before he smiles and lets her go.

"You better take care of Kimmy, Xan." Kirian narrows his eyes on me. "This is your first and only warning."

Both Kim and I grin as I ruffle his hair. "Sure will, Superman."

Seeming satisfied, he follows his father to where mine is sitting. Lewis's eyes are bright and shining as he watches us together. He might be Kim's biological father, but he always stayed as mine. Just like Calvin is hers.

Taking her hands in mine, I tug her close until I can smell her. Only, it's not perfume that seeps into my bones. It's the scent of summer—the grass and the pistachio gelato she was licking that day when we were six and she named me her knight.

It happened at this same park, under this same tree, when I knelt in front of her and she blessed me as her knight with a bamboo sword.

That's why she wanted to get married here. Kim said this place reminds her of the time she really wanted to be with me for good. The time she knew she'd always be my Green and I would always be her knight.

There isn't any better place for our eternal union.

My story with Kim might not have been the best. It could've gone differently, yes, but if it had, we wouldn't have met halfway as if it was meant to be.

She wouldn't have overcome her demons, the

mental abuse by her mother, and the depression that ate away at her soul.

Likewise, I wouldn't have been able to leave the shadow my mother left on my life or overcome my alcoholism issues. Today, I'm three years sober. Now and again, I drink diluted beverages and only when Kim is there, because she's the compass that sets me straight every time. Just like she did when we were eighteen.

Kim used to tell me that souls are attracted to each other and that my soul completes hers.

She's wrong. My soul doesn't complete hers. If it weren't for her, my soul would've been non-existent.

That's how deeply she impacts my life. That's how far gone I am for this woman.

Every day, I wake up and worship her body as a small show of how much she occupies my every waking and sleeping moment. She's grown more confident in herself and her body over the years. She once told me that I'm the best thing that could've happened to her.

It's the other way around.

Kimberly is the green of my life. The reason I'm standing right here without a fuckload of addictions hanging off my shoulders. If I hadn't found her again, I would've ended up just like my mother, roaming somewhere on earth, scamming people and begging for a drop of alcohol.

Kim saved me, and now I'll become her shield for the rest of our lives.

Still holding her hand in mine, I get on my knees. Murmurs break out amongst the crowd, but I ignore them. My sole attention is on the woman who's watching me with tears in her eyes.

"When we were six, you named me your knight, and I'd be honoured if you'd repeat that again, Green."

She grins, her eyes closing a little with her happiness as she releases one of my hands and taps me once on each shoulder. "You never stopped being my knight, Xan."

"And you never stopped being my Green, Kim."

NINE

Ronan

Age Twenty

There goes my plan to get married when I'm thirty-five—or forty. Seriously, I was even planning on staying a bachelor for life, like Lars.

But, hey, things don't always work as planned, do they?

One day, I was sitting in peace, smoking my weed, and then a wrecking ball in the form of a tiny woman barged into my life. And now I couldn't let her go, even if I wanted to.

See, Teal isn't just my fiancée—correction, my wife in a few minutes—she's also the one person I never knew I needed until I had her.

The one person who seeped through my flesh and caught me by the throat. Well, I'm the one who grabs her by the throat sometimes, but figuratively speaking, she's the one who does.

Xander keeps poking my side and waggling his brows at me, and I'm about ready to throw him in the pool. The only reason I don't is because no one but my Teal is allowed to be the main event today.

We opted for a wedding in my parents' mansion. I could tell you that Lars had a field day with all the preparations. He refused any wedding planners, saying they were amateurs and had no idea how things are actually done.

He turned the garden into a sitting area with lace ribbons decorating the trees and lights shining all over the pathways. Then he transformed the pool into a reception area. When Teal told him it was beautiful, he was like, "Of course it is. I made it happen."

She laughed and thanked him, and he grumbled as a form of reply before he disappeared inside—probably to write in his black book about how Teal lacks noble manners.

Mum helped with the entire process, not leaving Teal's side for even a second. Ever since she gained her health back and could move freely, she has made it her mission to be in on every moment of my life.

Dad, too, even though he's not forthcoming about it. We agreed that Mum would never know about Eduard the fucker, and I guess, ever since that scum's death, Dad and I have grown closer than before. It's like we're back to those times when I was a kid and I ran to him whenever I accomplished something exciting—or when Lars made me drink fucking milk.

Are we a perfect family? Far from it. But both my parents and Lars are the best family I could've asked for.

My gaze trails to the three of them sitting on the front row and I grin. Lars. *Sitting.* I know. I don't remember the last time I saw him rest his butt down. But I told him he's not allowed to stand during my wedding or I'll kick him out.

He bitched for some time in his snobbish tone, but obviously I won, because he complied.

Elsa walks down towards us with Knox by her side. He serves no role, except to piss off Aiden, who's glaring at him from his seat while Knox smiles from ear to ear.

After he delivers Elsa to her place as the maid of honour, he kisses her cheek and retreats. I'm surprised Aiden doesn't jump down his throat here and now.

Soon after, Teal appears with her hand tucked into Ethan's arm.

She's wearing a long black dress with a huge skirt and a lace bodice. Some people stop and stare at her unconventional choice, but my grin widens even more.

Putain.

That's exactly how I imagined *ma belle* when she said she would wear her favourite colour for her favourite day.

She told me that, in Spanish origins, wearing a black wedding dress means devoting the marriage until death.

I like that idea.

In fact, I like that idea so much that I would've been disappointed if she'd worn a normal white dress.

Teal isn't normal and she never will be. This is only further evidence of how deep and far she goes.

Nothing deters her from expressing her thoughts, and while that drives me insane sometimes, I can't get enough of her or her sarcastic comebacks. Or how she holds on to me as if I'm her world. As if she's as thrilled she found me as I am about finding her.

My favourite time of the day is when she crawls into my side and hugs me to sleep because it makes her feel safe.

My favourite part is when she says my name with that softness that she shows to no one but me.

My favourite meal is when she tries to cook something and makes me taste it first in case it's rubbish.

My favourite activity is when we run together and challenge each other on who gets to finish their lap first.

My favourite person is *her*.

I never thought I would allow someone so close, to the point they'd become my favourite. Or that they'd become the centre of my life.

But here we are and there she is.

Ma belle. My love. My all.

There was a moment in time where I hated myself and took refuge in other people. There was a moment in time where she shunned people and withdrew into herself.

And while sometimes those memories strike again, we don't run away from them anymore. I take her hand in mine and we talk to Dr Khan, Elsa's shrink whom she recommended to us.

At first, Teal didn't really want to talk, but now, she's even more opened up than me.

We talk about our coping mechanisms. About how she dealt with her trauma and how I dealt with mine.

We don't judge each other. Fuck anyone who judges how survivors deal with their trauma. Just because some treat it one way doesn't mean the entire world needs to do the same.

Trauma is a chronic illness that each human being deals with differently. Trauma is a cancer that can eat you from the inside out if you don't somehow come up with a coping mechanism.

Teal and I might have made mistakes, but that's how we learnt. That's how we got to this moment where we become one. Literally and figuratively.

It's not normal for two young people to get married at the age of twenty, but Teal and I were never the normal type.

We knew that early on and we own up to it. Besides, as she told me, we already know what we want, so what's the point of delaying it any further?

She has always been mine as much as I'm hers and there's no force in the world that will change that.

Before Ethan can give her to me, I snatch her close, my impatience getting the better of me. She smiles, her bright dark eyes shining with the motion.

"What do you think?" she whispers.

"I think you're mine till death, *ma belle*."

"And you're mine, Ronan."

I kiss her before the wedding even starts. Laughter

breaks out in the audience, but I couldn't give two fucks about them.

All of this is a formality. Teal and I always belonged together.

We just didn't know it at the time.

Now, we do.

Now, nothing will stop us from owning the world and leaving our gruesome experiences behind.

"I love you, Mrs Astor," I murmur against her mouth as I pull away.

She smiles in a soft, breathtaking way. "And I love you, Mr Astor."

TEN

Cole

Age Twenty-Eight

Chaos works in unpredictable patterns.

When I first met it after being kidnapped, I thought something was wrong with me and I needed to hide that something.

Until I walked to that park and saw it again.

Until I witnessed Silver in her truest, rawest form. It was a different type of chaos and I didn't feel the need to hide.

Not from her.

Never from her.

She's the one who saw my chaos and took it in both hands as if it was always hers to take.

She's the one who grabbed me, pushed me onto that bench, and straddled my lap so I wouldn't leave. Not that I could after that moment.

An invisible thread bound us together and there was no way in fuck anything could break it.

So what if we were siblings at one point? In my mind, she was mine before that even happened.

So what if she was engaged to that fucker Aiden first? It was never real. She and I are. In fact, we always were. It might have started when she cried her glitter tears on me or when she kissed my cheek for the first time or when she saved me all her firsts, just like I saved her mine.

"You didn't save me all your firsts," she told me the other day while we were lounging by the pool at her parents' house.

She was wearing her bikini and I was distracted, thinking of ways to have her remove it, but at the same time, I didn't want any of the staff to see her naked. I don't even like them seeing her in her bikini.

I adjusted my shades and tilted my book, *Calila e Dimna*. It was a special edition paperback she got for me on my birthday after the fucker Ronan burnt my previous one in a fit of jealousy. "Yes, I did."

"No, you didn't." She glared at me, and even though she was wearing huge Chanel shades, I could feel the maliciousness in her blue eyes. "After you kissed me when we were fourteen, you said I wasn't bad compared to the *others*."

I smiled. "You remember that."

"Of course I do, you wanker. It was my first kiss."

"It was my first kiss, too."

"But you said—"

"I only said that because you had your first waltz

with Aiden." My blood still boiled thinking about that. The fucker will pay for it for the rest of his life.

Silver's lips broke into a smile before she cleared her throat. "You…you're unbelievable."

"Is that supposed to be news, Butterfly?"

She removed her shades, revealing those deep blue eyes, then she abandoned her chair and straddled my lap, just like that day at the park. The view from beneath was the same—ethereal and breathtaking.

She slid my aviators away because, as she's always told me, she likes seeing my eyes—or rather, seeing herself in my eyes.

"So I was your first kiss," she murmured.

"You were."

She lifted her chin. "And last."

"And last." Then I devoured her until Cynthia joined us and cockblocked me.

She does that occasionally, cockblocks me just to see my reaction, and I do it to her every chance I get whenever she wants alone time with Sebastian.

What? I do hold grudges sometimes.

That's also why Aiden is my best man today. It's not because of his skills—which are terrible, by the way—but because I want him to see that Silver is mine. He might have been her fake fiancé at one time, and I can't erase that; however, I can make him watch me get married to her.

Not that he cares since he has Elsa, but this is a point I need to cement. During those years I thought she was his, I suffered in silence, and I don't want to ever have those feelings again. The feelings of being pushed into a corner until I couldn't sleep at night.

My thoughts come to a halt when Silver appears down the aisle, her gloved hand tucked into Sebastian's arm.

I admire how her wedding dress moulds to her curves as the sand shifts underneath her feet, leaving trails in their wake. My gaze ascends from the bottom to the top until I'm captured by bright eyes. She smiles at me in that shy yet determined way, like she used to do when we were young.

Our wedding is set on a small beach in the same French town where I first kissed her, held her hand, and walked with my palm on her back in front of people.

The first time where we were free, even though we'd suffered the loss of our unborn baby. The first time Silver kissed me without holding back. It was also when we got our tattoos together.

Now, we're commemorating those moments to memory once again. Only, now, it's in front of the world. We've been public for some time, but the marriage seals the deal once and for all.

It's been ten years. Ten fucking years since she became mine, and twenty years since I saw her at that park and decided she'd be my chaos.

But that's the thing about Silver, not only is she my chaos, but she's also my peace. The home I go back to every day.

We had to keep our relationship a secret for a long time, and while I enjoyed stealing her from the middle of people, tying her up or fucking her in dark corners,

I need the world to know the truth I've known since I was bloody eight years old.

Silver belongs to me as much as I belong to her.

The fact that I can finally shout it to the world fills me with a strange feeling I've never experienced before.

Giddiness? Nervousness?

Or maybe it's…happiness.

Before Silver, I didn't know what that word meant. After her, it simply means…my Butterfly. My chaos. My world.

She understands when I need a challenge and she doesn't shy away from meeting me head-on. That's what I love the most about Silver. The fact that she never backs away and never gives up. Actually, she needs the challenge as much as I do, and that's why she's the perfect woman for me.

And because she is, I intend to live the rest of our lives proving that fact.

Sebastian kisses his daughter on the cheek before he gives her to me. Her smile is still shy, but those blue eyes? Fuck, how they look at me.

I'm the one who's obsessed with seeing myself in her eyes, not the other way around. I'm the one who can't get enough of how they look at me.

"Notice something?" she whispers.

"What?"

"Nothing?" Her lips pull into an adorable pout.

"You should know by now that I notice everything about you." I motion at her dress's ribbon with the butterfly brooch on it. "Fucking butterflies."

"If you call them cockroaches with wings, I'll kill you."

I chuckle, tugging her to me because the distance between us is blasphemy. "They're bright and beautiful and make people happy, just like you, my Butterfly."

Her cheeks turn a deep shade of red. "Then you're more important than them, because you make me happy, Cole. You make me *so* happy."

"And I will continue to."

"Are we really getting married?" she whispers. "I still think it's a dream."

"Let's tie the knot here and I'll show you later whether or not it's a dream, Mrs Nash."

Her lips part and the urge to devour her hits me, so I do just that. I tie our own knot before anyone else can do it.

I'm hers.

She's mine.

PART THREE

The Honeymoon

ELEVEN

Astrid

"I can't keep up." I laugh as Levi takes my hand while we run through the rain.

Even though we always do this and I've gotten kind of used to standing under the rain when I'm in his company, I really can't keep up with his long athletic legs.

He's a football player, after all, and I still have no tolerance for physical activity, no matter how much Levi tries to implement that in me.

He stops, his fingers still intertwined with mine, and faces me, panting.

We're in Vegas.

No kidding.

When I told Levi the story about how my parents got married here and that I would love to visit it one day, he surprised me with a honeymoon in Vegas.

Sin City has never looked more sinful than when Levi is staring down at me with those deep blue eyes. His wet blond strands fall haphazardly across his forehead, shadowing his angular features and sharp jaw.

We've been here for a few days, and each one feels like a piece cut from paradise. I'm still not used to the fact that this man, who's the embodiment of a strong Viking, caring and protective, is actually my husband.

The dreamy days we've spent here, walking around and fucking in every corner, haven't helped, because since the wedding, I haven't had a chance to stop and soak in the fact that I belong to him as much as he belongs to me. That I'm now Astrid Elizabeth Clifford King. And my full name, although long as hell, is the best form it could ever be.

I haven't gotten the chance to watch him fall asleep and count his eyelashes or spy on him so I can sketch him later on.

Every day, he exhausts me to the point that I sleep in his arms like a kitten and only get up so he can whisk me off to a different adventure. It doesn't matter whether it's a casino, a restaurant, or the underground clubs where he can have me all for himself in dimly lit corners.

"Come on, Princess." He grins down at me, cradling my cheeks in his big hands, and tips my face up until my entire surroundings are filled with his presence. "Is that all you got?"

Despite our height difference, I get closer and run my fingers through his hair, submitting the golden strands to order. I've always loved the colour of his hair, and it's not just because he looks like a Viking. It's the only colour that would suit him. Although the other

King men, Jonathan and Aiden, have dark hair, Levi has a light shade, and that alone shows how special he is. He's cut from an extraordinary cloth to be solely mine.

"I miss you," I murmur.

Still clutching my cheeks, he taps my nose with his thumb. "I've been here the entire time."

"I miss you, even when you're close. That's crazy isn't it?"

He shakes his head once. "I'm the same. I miss you when I can't breathe you. When I can't hear your voice or touch you. I miss you when I think I have to leave you."

"Levi…"

"So don't let me miss you. I turn grumpy as fuck when I do, and that's not good for anyone who's near me at the time."

"I won't if you don't let me miss you."

"That's out of the question. Not even when you're old and grey and sick of me, Princess."

I stare at him through my vision that's blurred by the rain. "I'll never get sick of my husband."

His grin widens until a spark lights up the deep blue of his eyes. "I like that."

"How I won't get sick of you?"

"That, too, but also the part where you call me your husband, wife."

"I like it, too."

He leans over and brushes his nose against mine. "I guess this means I need to consummate our marriage."

"You already did. Multiple times."

"Multiple times, huh? Have you been counting, Princess?"

"As if I could ever keep up." My cheeks heat, recalling all the positions he took me in. "You fucked me everywhere."

"Not under the rain."

And with that, he lifts me in his arms. I squeal as he runs with me wrapped all around him.

My fingers grip his shoulders tight as I laugh with utter delight.

Best honeymoon ever.

TWELVE

Elsa

When Aiden mentioned that Jonathan owned an island, I thought he was kidding.

Far from it.

I should've known that my father-in-law, Jonathan King, is more than capable of owning an island. It shouldn't even have come as a surprise.

It's where we opted to spend the honeymoon, and I have no doubt that this is another of Aiden's methods to have me completely for himself.

Not that I'm complaining.

During the wedding preparations, I barely got a glimpse of him. I was always surrounded by Kim, Teal, Astrid, Knox, and even Silver, who helped me with picking the dress.

The fact that Kim forgave her didn't leave me any reason to stay mad at Silver. Especially after the drunken talk we had one night about all that happened during Royal Elite's final years.

Silver only ever had eyes for Cole, and my jealousy of her was uncalled for. Seems like Aiden isn't the only possessive one with an irrational streak. Besides, I still feel bad for hitting her that time at Aiden's house when she never attacked me.

After I found out that she suspected she was pregnant at the time, I apologised and she apologised for everything else—especially for turning her back on Kim, despite secretly checking in on her.

Since then, Silver and I have belonged to the same circle of friends. We have Teal and Kim in common, after all.

So because of the lively atmosphere during the wedding preparations, I didn't really get my fill of Aiden. And the girls spent the night before the ceremony with me so that he couldn't sneak in and see me before the big day.

Not that it stopped him. He stood under my balcony and sent me a few texts that made me grin like an idiot.

Aiden: Last night apart, sweetheart.

Elsa: We already live together.

Aiden: Doesn't count. You don't have my last name.

Elsa: Is that important?

Aiden: Fuck right, it is. You're officially mine,

sweetheart, and you won't leave my side like you did when we were eight.

Elsa: Aiden…I didn't remember at the time. Are you going to hold a grudge about that for eternity?

Aiden: I will never hold a grudge against you as long as you're by my side, sweetheart.

I went to sleep with a smile on my face at his words. In a way, I knew Aiden didn't like that I forgot about him, and because it still hurts him in some way, I'll spend the rest of my life purging that pain away.

Just because he's some sort of a sociopath doesn't mean he doesn't get hurt. It only means that he chooses different methods to act upon it.

Currently, we stand at the top of a waterfall, overlooking the most hypnotising turquoise sea I've ever seen.

The water cascades down below, meeting the surface with a *sploosh*.

"Whoa." I snap pictures from all different angles. "This is mesmerising. Who knew Jonathan has such good taste."

"He doesn't." Strong arms wrap around my waist from behind as Aiden rests his chin at the top of my head. "He won it over poker."

"Still, he owns it."

"Which means I own it, too."

I smile, still snapping pictures. Aiden doesn't like me expressing awe towards anyone, even if it's his forty-four-year-old dad. Not that I would ever get close to

Jonathan. He's still terrifying as hell and he very much holds a grudge against my dad—and me, by extension.

Aiden snatches my phone away and throws it on top of the small bag we brought with us for the hike.

"Hey!" I turn around against his chest. "I was using that."

"Not anymore." His expression remains the same. "Besides, are you here for the pictures or for me?"

"The pictures." I hide my mischievous grin. "Definitely the pictures."

"You're playing with fire, sweetheart."

I stare up at his deep grey eyes and his angular features that only keep sharpening over time. The Aiden from Royal Elite School might've been handsome, but now, he's lethal. Knowing that he'll probably grow up to have the merciless beauty of his father, I can't help but feel giddy to be with him every step of the way.

We've already lost ten years of our lives apart. There will be no more wasting time.

I stand on tiptoes and brush my lips against his. "I thought playing with fire came with being yours."

"Fuck." His hold tightens around my waist. "You're everything I could've asked for."

"And you are mine."

"Even when I piss you off?"

I sigh. "Even when you piss me off. I don't only love your protective side, Aiden. I fell in love with everything about you."

Aiden rests his forehead against mine so that I'm captured in his grey irises. "You were made for me, sweetheart."

"And you were made for me."

His eyes glint with sadism. "Do you trust me?"

"Absolutely."

Aiden grabs me tight and drags me to the edge. I shriek as we fall all the way down.

It's not fear that takes me over. It's complete, utter excitement because by being in Aiden's arms, I have no doubt that everything will be fine.

He said I saved him once upon a time.

What he doesn't know is that he saved me, too.

THIRTEEN

Kimberley

When Xan said we'd spend our honeymoon in a castle, I didn't think it would be an *actual* castle. No clue how he even got us this whole mansion all to ourselves.

This area of Yorkshire has a lot of castles due to the wars that happened in the Middle Ages, but there's something special about this one.

I run up the stairs, half escaping Xan's merciless clutches, and half attempting to find out why I have an intuition that it's a special castle.

My feet come to a halt when I reach the top, and it's not because of the breathtaking view of the fields below—although that does play a part.

It's the whole image of the high towers and the terrace. The stone railings and the smooth floor, which give a nostalgic view.

Everything is so familiar.

A hard body crashes into me from behind and I squeal as I lose my footing. Xan wraps his strong arms around my waist, steadying me in place as he spins me around to face him.

He's breathing heavily, probably due to the run up the old stairs. I, on the other hand? I cease breathing altogether.

For a moment in time, I get lost in the deep magical blue of his eyes, in the rebellious blond strands falling all over his forehead, in the way he's holding me close, as if he's afraid to let me go.

I wind my arms around his lean waist because, in a way, I'm also scared of losing him. The thought of not having him in my life after I finally found him again gives me nightmares sometimes. The type he holds me through and coaxes me to completely forget about.

He raises a perfect brow. "You thought you could escape me, Green?"

"I wasn't escaping."

"Not that you could with these short legs."

"Hey!"

"Or your stamina."

"I've been working on improving it!"

"You mean *we've* been working on improving it." He winks.

My cheeks flame and I stare to the side. "Shut up."

He places two fingers underneath my chin and switches my attention back to him. "Did I tell you that you're so fucking adorable when you're shy?"

"I'm not a kid anymore."

"No, you're not. Doesn't mean you're any less

adorable, Green." He pinches my cheek and I swat his hand away as I fight the blood rushing to my face.

His attention remains on me as a beautiful, heart-stopping smile grazes his lips. It doesn't matter how many times I see that smile or how long I spend with him. The way those dimples make an appearance will always be my weakness. I can't resist stopping and staring and probably looking like an idiot.

This man is now my husband.

My. Husband.

The man I will share the rest of my life with.

I'm so lucky that I found him when we were young. We had a connection before we even knew what a connection meant. The whole separation in between, although cruel, morphed us into who we are today and I wouldn't have it any other way.

Neither of us are perfect, but we fit perfectly. After RES, we built back our relationship from the past. Even though we don't agree on everything, we don't clash. We don't stay mad at each other for too long.

Every night, we crawl back into each other's arms and sigh as we fall asleep.

It's even better than all the romance novels I've read. Those are fictional, but my Xan is real.

Very real.

He's the most real thing in my life and nothing will take that away.

"Green!"

"Huh?" *Was he speaking?*

"I asked why you came up here?"

"Oh, it's…the view."

"The view?"

"The castle. Doesn't it look like it's from one of those children's books I got from Nana?"

He grins wide, his dimples deepening. "You noticed that."

"You did it on purpose?"

He feigns a curtsy. "Your knight is always at your service, my queen."

"God." I can't help smiling like an idiot. It must've taken him a lot of digging to find something remotely similar to what we used to read together.

I palm his cheek, thumb stroking his skin. "I'm so lucky to have you."

"It's the other way around. I'm the lucky bastard because you're in my life, because you forgave all my fuckups and chose me. I'll spend the rest of my life making it up to you, Green. After all, you staked your claim on me when you named me your knight."

"And now, I'm Mrs Knight."

"I love my last name on you."

"Me, too."

He brushes his lips against mine, and although it's brief, my breathing hitches and I snuggle further into the hard ridges of his body. There was too much distance between us in the past and there's no way I'll let that repeat.

But even with the distance, we saw each other. We felt each other's darkness and demons, and I think that's why we're inseparable now.

That's why we appreciate each moment spent in

each other's embrace. We take nothing for granted, because life is meant to be lived to its fullest.

"Do you know that I love you, Green?"

I laugh. "You kind of tell me every day."

"It's not enough. Nothing is enough when I'm with you. Now say it."

"What?"

"That you love me, too."

"What if I stopped?"

"You won't."

"Arrogant much, Xan?"

"No, but I will fight for your love all over again if I have to."

"As if I would ever stop loving you. My heart and my soul are yours, Xan. They always were."

"You forgot something."

"What?"

"Your body is also mine."

I squeal, then break down in giggles as he lifts me in his arms and throws me on the wooden bench.

Here we go again.

FOURTEEN

Teal

"**R**eady, *ma belle?*"

No.

I'm far from being ready. Actually, I want to crawl back to our hotel room.

Instead of sounding like a coward, I rub Ronan's bicep slowly, which has become my sign for when I want him to fuck me.

Though I don't really get to use it a lot, because he's usually ready before I have to tell him anything.

I rise on my tiptoes to whisper in his ear, "Let's go back to the hotel and you can have three rounds."

His eyes darken, and I feel his bulge growing against my stomach.

I'll never get used to how easily I can turn Ronan on. Sometimes, it only takes a touch and he's more than ready to ravage me senseless, even in public places.

Not here, though.

We're standing on the top of the Colossus Bridge near Milan and there are too many people for him to act on his desire.

"Fuck, *belle*," he mutters under his breath. "When did you decide to take cocktease as a job?"

Since I got to know him, but I don't say that. Instead, I run my fingers over the hard muscles of his chest and down to his waist, making him groan.

He grabs both of my hands in one of his own and imprisons them at his chest. A sly smile grazes his lips. "Are you scared?"

"No!"

"Are you sure, though?"

"Yes."

"Hmm, why do I feel like you're seducing me just so you can escape this."

"Hmph. This is child's play. I am not scared, Ron."

"Uh-huh."

"Stop it." I glare up at him, and that merely makes him widen his smile.

Sometimes, I hate how easily he can read through all my layers. He's the only person who sees past the persona I project onto the world and senses the vulnerable part in me. The part I usually keep under lock and key because I don't want it to get hurt by the harsh outside world.

With Ronan, though, I want to display it and let him feast on it. Despite his jokester personality, he has so much empathy, it's insane.

It makes me want to protect him, too, because the

world is too cruel for someone like him. The world doesn't deserve a pure soul like Ronan.

He grabs my cheeks with his hands so that we're staring into each other's eyes. I'm so tiny compared to him and I hate that he has so much height on me, I have to stand on my tiptoes to get to his face—or close enough.

Whenever he does this, the entire world disappears from around us. The only one I see is him.

The only thing I feel is his body glued to mine, even though the vest and ropes are in the way.

"Do you trust me?" he murmurs in the tone that turns me boneless every time.

"With my life."

"Time to test that, *ma belle.*"

Ugh. I must've been drunk when I agreed to this. Oh, wait, I was. But not on alcohol. I was completely spent last night after he wrenched multiple orgasms out of me. So when he suggested we go bungee jumping today, I might've agreed while half-asleep.

Ronan, being a manipulative arsehole when it suits him, took that opportunity and brought us here first thing in the morning.

"How about five rounds?"

He grins. "Okay."

"Okay?"

"I will have those rounds as soon as we go back, *trésor.*"

"No. You don't get the rounds if you make me do this."

"What if I change your mind?"

"You can't change my mind."

"If you like this, if you let go and scream, then I will get my rounds."

I poke his side. "So now they're *your* rounds?"

"They always were." He winks, and I can't help but smile.

Ronan will be Ronan. He's addicted to adrenaline and fun. Although we're both moving on from the trauma of our pasts, Ronan has never changed into a grim person.

He's still the heart of the party and the one people gravitate towards. I'm one of those people, but the difference is that he somehow gravitates towards me, too.

He somehow can't fall asleep unless I'm by his side, holding him close. He somehow only searches for me.

He's somehow mine.

My husband. My world.

He's everything I could've asked for and more. I might be addicted to him. The thought of waking up to find him gone gives me nightmares.

So whatever. I don't care if it's bungee jumping or literal jumping. I'd go anywhere with this man.

Hell included.

I wrap my arms around his waist, holding on to him because he's the only anchor I've ever needed in my life.

"That's my woman." He leans his head down and captures my mouth in a kiss.

I get lost in the softness of his lips, in the way his entire body angles towards me. My eyes close as I soak in the overwhelming sensation. The way Ronan kisses is like he's saying without words that he can't get enough of me as much as I can't get enough of him.

His lips slowly leave mine and I open my eyes to stare at his dark ones.

"Why do I love you so much, Ronan?" I sigh.

His grin is to die for. It's so bright and happy and I want to keep it that way for a lifetime. He holds me to him by the waist. "Because I won you over, *belle*."

And then we jump. Arms around each other, hearts beating loudly against one another.

And in the air, when we're both falling and gazing into each other's eyes, a sense of freedom hits me in the bones.

The freedom of being with this man until death do us part.

FIFTEEN

Silver

I moan as the soft sea breeze hits my body.

My nipples peak and I rub my thighs together. That's when I realise I have nothing on.

No clothes.

My eyes shoot open, wrenching me from sleep, and sure enough, I'm lying on the chaise longue under the sun, completely naked.

Cole.

No one other than that pervert would remove my clothes. I hate that the part I'm the most bothered about is that I wasn't fully awake to witness it.

Groaning, I get up on my elbows to search for my husband.

I smile to myself.

Cole is my husband. It took us ten years since we got together and twenty years since we promised each other our firsts, but we're finally here.

We're married.

We're spending our honeymoon in France, in that small town where we first kissed each other in public. The town where we got our tattoos together.

My fingers snake over my side to touch the butterfly I got that day. Although a bit impulsive, that was one of the best decisions I've made in my life.

Aside from marrying the love of my life. The peace of my days and the absolute chaos in others.

But I wouldn't change anything about him, even if I could.

We're currently on a yacht, sailing through the Mediterranean Sea. And yes, Cole owns a yacht. I think I underestimated William Nash's fortune, because apparently, even though he passed away a long time ago, he spent his life building a literal empire of gold.

It's become even better ever since Cole struck a partnership with both Jonathan King, Aiden's father, and Ethan Steel, Elsa's father. He knows exactly which bigwigs to target. With his calculative personality, he was made for the business world.

And my competitive personality is also fit for it. I can't wait for Cole and me to conquer the world, or as he says, to *own* it.

We'll have a problem with Aiden, considering his own competitive streak, but he stands no chance if Cole and I come at him full force.

That arsehole is going down.

I don't bother searching for clothes as I stand up. We're alone on the yacht, and although it's not currently moving, there are no people in sight. We're literally in the middle of nowhere, where no one knows us and we can be ourselves.

Not that it would cause a problem if we were together in public. After all, we got married.

But, in a way, we yearn for our private time together, to do the freaky stuff only the two of us know. Cole still ties me up and wrenches one explosive orgasm after the other from me. We still go to *La Débauche* to watch other people have sex while we get each other off.

We still sneak to dark corners for quickies because my husband can't keep his hands off me—just like I can't keep my hands off him.

"Cole?" I call, but there's no reply.

I search downstairs and in the rooms, but there's no sign of him. I return upstairs, my fingers shaking the slightest bit.

I try telling myself that he's probably in the captain's cabin, considering that he's the one who personally sails the yacht, but my heart won't stop beating loud and fast.

After everything that happened between us, I don't like spending time apart from Cole. Not that he ever stays away from me. He's my shadow most of the time and rarely gives me an opportunity to miss him.

Now, however, there's no trace of him.

I stand at the railing and peek over. That's when I see him. In the sea, floating with his head facing down.

My heart hammers when he doesn't move. *No, no...*

Cole might have had that trauma in the pool of his old house, but he's an excellent swimmer outside of that.

Why isn't he moving?

I don't think about it as I jump. Cold water shocks my skin and fills my nostrils, but I don't pause as I reach for him. By the time I touch him, he's surfaced, his wet hair sticking to his forehead and his deep green eyes glinting in the sun.

I hit his shoulder, breathing heavily. "You fucking arsehole! I thought something had happened to you."

He holds me to his chest, causing my hits to die out. "And leave you? You think that would be possible?"

I breathe in his cinnamon scent, taking my fill of him. "Don't ever do that again."

"I was only observing under the sea. I didn't think you'd wake up so soon from your nap."

"Well, you took my clothes, you pervert."

"It takes one to know one, Butterfly."

"What the hell are you talking about?"

"You think I don't notice when you take pictures of me when I'm asleep?"

"I-I do not."

"Do you stare at them when I'm not beside you? Do you have another kink I should know about? You know I'm always game for making all your kinky wishes come true."

That he is. There hasn't been any wish that he hasn't made come true. He lights my body on fire in the best way possible, and he doesn't stop until I'm so utterly spent and pleased.

"Ready whenever you are." He thrusts his thigh between mine, making me feel his erection, and yup, he's also naked.

"Is this why you removed my bikini?"

"No, I was merely being a good sport so you won't have tan lines, not that anyone would see them." He lowers his head and sucks on the tender flesh of my breast, leaving a hot red mark.

I arch my back, my eyes closing. This has always been our favourite parts; he loves marking me in places only he can see and I love staring at the marks he leaves on my body.

He lifts his head and his eyes hold mine hostage. I'm constantly in awe of the way he looks at me, the way he wants me, the way he never stares at anyone else but me.

It's not just about the sex or the kinks, it's about how he holds me to him for no reason other than to feel me near. It's about how he reads to me every night with my head lying on his lap, and if I fall asleep, he hugs me close and sleeps with his lips sealed to my forehead.

It's about him and me and the long journey we took so we could finally be together in front of the whole world.

I wind my arms around his neck and stroke the hairs at his nape. "You're my world, Cole."

"I know."

"No, I mean it. You're my entire world and I don't know how I'd ever be able to live in it without you."

"You won't have to, because you won't be able to get rid of me, Butterfly. You're my chaos, remember?"

"And your calm?"

"And my calm."

"And your love?"

He smiles, and I nearly faint here and now. "And my love."

"I love you so much. Now and forever, husband."

"And I love you, wife."

PART FOUR

The Pregnancy

SIXTEEN

Levi

Age Twenty-Three

I throw my bag on the sofa and head to the kitchen to grab some water.

The practice was fucking exhausting today. I satisfied my usual need for adrenaline and more.

Now, I just want to snuggle with my beautiful wife and watch one of those gory films she loves so much. Other women enjoy romcoms, but mine is obsessed with weird shit. I love her even more for her eclectic taste.

After taking a sip of water, I stop with the bottle half-way to my mouth. The door to the art studio is open.

Usually when I return home early, I have to mope in front of it like a fucking idiot until she comes out. I respect her need for alone time so that she can create masterpieces. Besides, Astrid always says I'm distracting, so I try to stay out of the way. The keyword being 'try'.

The fact that the door is now open is wrong. I place the

bottle on the counter and go inside. Did Daniel come by? But he's in the States. He and Knox, Ronan's brother-in-law, formed some sort of friendship that's based on shagging their way through the American female population and decided to stay in the States even after they finished college. Astrid would've told me if Daniel was coming back, and even if she hadn't, I would've sensed it, considering she spends the entire week out of her skin with excitement.

That means Daniel is out of the way.

I don't think it's Elsa or my uncle's wife either since they're with Aiden and Jonathan at the latter's island. Astrid and I skipped because I had practice and Astrid was…unwell.

That's what she told Aurora, my uncle's wife, when she talked to her on the phone last night. I vaguely remember the word 'unwell' and I thought it was a dream.

My feet are heavy as I step into the art studio. The smell of paint and charcoal hits my nostrils, and I stop at the threshold to catch my breathing.

It's nothing. It'll be nothing.

My Astrid is stronger than the world and everything in it. There's no way she's *that* unwell.

I stop when I find her standing in front of the mirror. She has one here for when she sketches my nudes. She says it's so she can get all possible angles. Usually, I end up fucking her in front of it because I want her to see us from all possible angles.

Right now, though, she doesn't seem to be sketching or anything.

Her face is pale as she holds her tank top to

underneath her breasts and gazes at the mirror with a blank stare.

"Astrid…" I murmur, my voice low and translating the turmoil that's whirling inside me.

She startles before she releases her tank top and faces me, a faint smile on her face. It's still pale, her cheeks missing all their colour.

I reach her in two steps and cup her chin, then look at her intently. Has she been getting sick and I didn't notice it?

That shouldn't happen. I watch her more than I watch anything in this world—myself included.

Her well-being comes before anything else.

"What's wrong, Princess?"

"I didn't hear you come in." She's still smiling.

"Don't try to escape this. What's wrong with you?"

"Why would you think there's something wrong with me?"

"Because you're not painting and you're pale and you told Aurora you're fucking unwell. Fuck." I run a hand through my hair. "I should've noticed it before."

"I don't think you could've. Not when I didn't know myself." She takes my hand, making me release my hair, and smooths the strands with her other palm.

This is why Astrid is my calm. She doesn't allow me to get sucked into the black hole that only manages to push me into a vicious cycle. She always pulls me away before I'm dragged inside.

"You didn't know what?" I ask in a barely audible voice. My shoulder blades snap together with fucking fear. The thought that something could happen to her drives me bonkers.

I just need to know what it is so I can fix it. Surely Jonathan can threaten a doctor or two, or an entire fucking hospital, if needed.

"Don't be agitated, Lev. I only confirmed it this morning."

"Confirmed what?"

She swallows, her delicate throat moving with the motion.

"Princess, I'm barely holding on here, so any day now."

"I'm pregnant."

The words reach my ears, but it takes me a few seconds to absorb them. "So you're not sick?"

"Sick? No. I have some nausea, but it's nothing bad."

"Right."

"Right?" She scowls, her brow furrowing. "That's all you have to say? Aren't you…happy?"

"Of course I am, but I'm happier that you're healthy, Princess. I nearly lost my heart thinking you were sick or some shit. Are you healthy?"

She bites her lower lip. "I think so. We need to go to the doctor since I only took a few tests."

I hold her hand. "Let's go right now. I'll ask Aiden for Elsa's OB-GYN. If she can handle Aiden's late night calls, she can handle mine."

"Wait." She tugs on my fingers, making me stop and face her again. "Aren't you mad that this happened without a plan? We wanted to wait, and then this came along. I think it's because of that one time I missed the pill."

"Why would I be mad, Princess?" I place my hand on her stomach, and even though there's no bump or anything, I feel a sense of belonging already. "As long as you're happy, I'm more than ready for this. Are you? Happy, I mean?"

She nods frantically, holding on to my hand that's on her stomach. "I didn't know I wanted this so badly until I saw the positive line on the test. I want to be the mother of your children, Levi."

I grin. "The mother of my children. I like that."

"You do?"

"Fuck right, I do." I kiss her lips to the point that she's breathless when I release her. "Now, let's make sure you're healthy."

SEVENTEEN

Elsa

Age Twenty-One

"As I was saying, you can't argue with me using some theory. Be an actual nerd and prove it in real time."

Aiden stares at our classmates with his signature poker face. I swear he's become even more tenacious about hiding his emotions.

I'm lucky I met him at eighteen, because twenty-one-year-old Aiden would've driven me bonkers.

Scratch that. He does, but I know him well enough to counter him at every turn now. I don't always win, but the challenge is worth it.

Our colleagues stare at him with questions and no answers.

Only Aiden would call university students nerds

to their faces. When I told him not to do that, he said he's a firm believer in calling things by their names.

"Anyone?" he challenges. "Yeah, I didn't think so."

He's lucky Cole isn't here. It would've morphed into a full-blown war if he was, and we'd be all sitting here watching them argue all night.

No one ever wins, but Aiden keeps insisting he takes it easy on him.

"Actually, there's one." A sinister voice comes from my right. His American accent differentiates him immediately.

I groan even before the twat joins the circle. I thought we were lucky tonight since Cole had things to take care of.

Turns out, no.

"What are you even doing here?" I ask. "You don't belong to this club."

"I do now." Deep green eyes fill with mischief as he waves his access card. "I had to be where all the cool kids go. Isn't that right, Pres?"

Our debate club president, Oliver, nods at the American's charming grin.

I roll my eyes. The only reason he joined is to challenge Aiden and Cole. I swear they attract lunatics like this American as if they were magnets.

Even Aiden didn't join the club out of goodwill. I joined first and he just slid in because 'he was interested'.

Interested, my arse. More like he wants to be here to shoo the flies away, as he calls them.

Aiden's possessiveness knows no limits. He

doesn't like how close I am to the other club members, so he barged in to make their lives hell. He can be so frustratingly argumentative when he chooses to.

"Good of you to join us, Ash." Aiden grins as sadism sparks in his eyes. "Now look away from my wife before I create a diplomatic problem between England and the US."

The all-American golden boy bursts into laughter, raising his hands. "All right, all right. You have it bad, dude."

Aiden wraps his hand around mine, interlacing our fingers as if to prove a point.

Our rings are above each other's. Something Aiden likes to do a lot.

We've been married for two years, and he's been publicising it everywhere. Whenever someone stares in my direction, he nearly blinds them with the huge diamond ring he got for me.

It's not something I would wear, but I accepted it nonetheless. This ring was Alicia's, and I understand its emotional value for Aiden.

I soon found out he's also using it to mark his territory at every opportunity.

The press is the only medium he didn't use for publicity, but he didn't need to.

Our wedding, although exclusive to family and friends, made the headlines.

The King and Steel marriage was written about over and over in business columns and newspapers.

It's the start of a new era for both companies.

While Dad and Jonathan aren't the best of friends, they learned to work together.

I still can't trust Agnus completely. He really is a psychopath and I'm always wary of him. However, Dad trusts him even though he seems to know of his exact nature.

Agnus plays a huge part in Dad and Jonathan's partnership. He's become a pillar of strength for our families, and I can't hate him for that.

Even Aunt and Uncle's company, Quinn Engineering, has been thriving since the partnership between King Enterprise and Steel Corporation.

Aunt was a little sad when I chose Oxford over Cambridge, but she quickly got over it.

"Do you have anything to add to the discussion, Ash?" Aiden asks his American friend.

All the team members focus on the latter.

Some girls blush. Others stare up at him with dreamy eyes.

If only they knew what lurks under the beautiful façade.

He's just like Aiden. If not a little more unhinged. I still have no idea why he left his prestigious college back in the States to join us here.

"Yes, actually." He flops into a chair, his arms hanging off the edge. "See, Aiden. I don't have to prove it to you because we're not under legal obligation. I can choose to prove it, but it's only voluntary."

"When does voluntary end and the obligation start?" Aiden shoots back.

They go on and on. The audience are watching

two titans clash with gaped mouths. Even the president doesn't dare to say anything.

Me, on the other hand? I'm done watching two sociopaths trying to outsmart one another.

As Asher goes on and on about legal texts and whatnot, I squeeze Aiden's hand and whisper, "I'm tired. Let's go home."

He doesn't even stop to consider it.

Still clutching my hand, he stands, taking me up with him and effectively cutting off Asher. "My wife needs to rest."

"Loser," Asher mutters.

Aiden smirks. "I'm taking a rain check."

"I'll be here," Asher calls to our backs as we head to the door. "Now, where was I?"

He launches into a long, one-sided argument.

"Why are you even friends with him?" I ask as soon as we're alone.

"Because he's fun, sweetheart. We need fun people who aren't politically correct."

"You mean sociopaths."

"Every society needs old-fashioned villains." He grins down at me, then his brows crease. "Why are you tired?"

"I'm—"

Before I can say anything, he slams his palm on the middle of my chest.

"Aiden!" I watch our surroundings. I know he's just checking my heartbeat—like he does every day. Actually, he sometimes sleeps with his head on my heart to make sure it's working properly.

"I told you to check my wrist pulse when we're in public," I whisper. "People are watching."

"Fuck people. I'll check my wife's pulse any way I like." He removes his hand and places two fingers on my neck. "Hmm. Your pulse is fine."

"It is," I say as we step into the cold air.

"Then what is it? Do you feel chest tightness?"

"No."

"Palpitations?"

I shake my head.

Aiden is strict as fuck when it comes to my health. He's more religious about my appointments than I am. He's continuously studying about heart conditions like doctors with degrees.

He's even considering taking a second course in medicine.

No kidding, he really is.

He steps in front of me, buttons my coat to my chin, removes his scarf and ties it snugly around my neck.

It smells of him, clean and masculine. I take a deep inhale, breathing him into my lungs.

Aiden takes my cold hand in his and blows warm air into them before he places them in my pockets.

I watch him with a smile on my face. This side of Aiden always gets me in a knot. He's so caring and attentive, I actually have nightmares about a life without him.

He's become such a constant I can't breathe without anymore.

Forget love and adoration, Aiden is fucking air to me. He's everything I want in life and more. For that reason alone, I move onto my tiptoes and plant a kiss on his lips.

He grins with boyish charm.

Aiden likes it when I surprise him with kisses or when I demand pleasure. He says it turns him on more than anything else.

"Come on, it's cold." He pulls on my cheek. "I need to get my wife home."

Right. Home.

Our place is about a fifteen minutes' drive from campus.

We spend it talking about classes while Aiden has his hand up my thigh. I'm lucky to be wearing jeans; if I was in a skirt, he'd be bringing me to orgasm by now.

Aiden is still Aiden. Boundless and shameless.

He drives me crazy. I swear I fall for him a little more every day. I fall in love with how he prepares breakfast for me every morning. How he takes me on a run and watches my heart rate through it. How he carries me to bed from my desk every night when I fall asleep on it. How he fucks me as if he can't get enough of me.

I love his attentiveness and his protectiveness. Hell, I even love his possessiveness sometimes.

I love all of him.

We arrive at our place.

It's a two-storey house with a small garden I take care of. Aiden bought the land next to us for our one-year anniversary. He said it's a gift so I can build my first house.

Our actual house.

I've been going crazy since then, coming up with a thousand and one ideas. I'm even contemplating combining the two lands and having a blast with it.

For now, we live in a cosy house with an antique feel to it.

As soon as we're inside, I stop to remove my coat. Aiden yanks off his jacket and jogs to the kitchen—for my meds, no doubt.

I study our house, the wooden flooring and the dark decor.

A tinge of arousal hits me at the memory of Aiden taking me in every corner of this house. On the sofa, against the counter, and even on the floor near the entrance.

This place is filled with so many heart-warming memories.

After hanging the coat and scarf onto the hook on the wall, I tiptoe towards the kitchen. Aiden stands at the counter fussing with pills. He still reads the label every time. There's no risk of error with him.

I wrap my arms around him from behind and rub my cheek against his back.

Aiden might not be a football player anymore—except for the occasional games now and then—but his physique is still hard and toned.

We go on runs together and he works out when he has insomnia, although it's become rare since our marriage.

"What do you want most in the world, Aiden?"

"You." He doesn't even miss a beat.

I smile. "What else?"

"You healthy and happy and fucking mine."

God. This man will be the death of me.

"What else?"

"That's all."

"That's all?"

"Yes." He spins around and hands me the pills with a glass of water.

I swallow the meds as he watches me intently. I watch him, too. His tousled, inky hair, the mole on the corner of his metal eyes, and the hint of his arrow tattoos as the sleeve of his shirt bunches up.

He clutches my elbow. "Let's get you some rest."

I squirm free. "I'm not tired."

He raises an eyebrow and tilts his head. "If you're not tired, I'll fuck you in the shower like yesterday. I like it when you are horny, climbing up my body and clawing at my back."

"There's a reason for that."

"Whatever it is, I like the reason. Let's repeat it today." He grins and goes back to fiddling with the pills.

I take a deep breath. Okay, here goes.

"Aiden?"

"Hmm, sweetheart?"

"I'm pregnant. Six weeks, to be exact."

He freezes, the bottle of pills half-suspended in his hands.

Aiden wanted a kid three years ago, but he

completely backed off when Dr Albert said it could be a danger to my life at that stage.

However, three months ago, Dr Albert told me it's now safe for me to have a child. Since then, I've been without birth control. I wanted to give him a surprise on our second anniversary two months ago. But I didn't fall pregnant.

I nearly cried every time my period came on time for the past three months.

Yesterday, my period was two weeks late. I took a test and boom, pregnant. I was so happy, I wanted to tell Aiden right away, but I kept it to myself until I had tests done with both Dr Albert and an OB-GYN.

Aiden spins back around. My mouth falls open. I never expected to see that expression on Aiden's face.

Fear.

Complete terror.

He grabs my arm. "Let's go to Dr Albert. He'll tell us how to deal with this—"

"No." I wiggle away from him. "I'm having this child."

"And I'm not having a child that will risk your life." Aiden's voice is authoritative and final. "I'd rather be childless than without you."

My eyes fill with tears at his statement, because I know it's true. Aiden would be happy with just me by his side. I feel it in my soul.

But I want to give him more. I want to give him everything. I want to be the mother of his children.

"I'm not in danger." I cradle his cheek with my palm. "I talked to Dr Albert and the OB-GYN, and we had tests done. The baby and I are healthy."

He narrows his eyes. "Are you just saying that so I'd change my mind?"

"I know you'd barge into Dr Albert's house to make sure my words are correct, so no, I'm not bluffing. I have the test results and everything in my bag."

He jogs to it and spends minutes reading the papers over and over again. I stand there watching him, waiting for his reaction.

He switches his gaze to stare at the ultrasound scan of a small life. A life he and I created.

"So?" I ask carefully. "What do you think?"

"You're pregnant." He stares between me and the ultrasound scan as if to make sure.

"Yes, Aiden." I cradle my stomach. "I'm carrying your baby."

"You're carrying my baby," he repeats, slowly approaching me.

When he's within touching distance, I take his hand and place it on my stomach.

It's still flat, but I can feel the life humming inside me. I can already feel the connection.

He stares at his hand and slowly strokes my stomach.

"We created a life, Aiden," I murmur. "Are you happy?"

He rips his gaze from my stomach to meet my eyes. "Are you?"

"I'm over the moon. This is the best gift you could've given me." I press my lips to his. "I love you."

He wraps his arms around me and I squeal as he lifts me off the ground and hugs me. My arms wind around him as he kisses my mouth, my cheeks, my nose, and my forehead.

"You're the best gift I've ever been given, my queen."

"And you're mine, my king."

EIGHTEEN

Xander

Age Twenty-Six

You know that feeling where you love someone so much that you'd kill for them, but sometimes, you want to kill them?

Those tiny moments where you want to strangle them while you fuck them?

This is one of those times.

Those thoughts have never stopped swirling in my head since the company dinner we had at Ronan's house.

And now, Kim is walking by my side, interlacing her fingers with mine as if nothing happened.

We'll see about that.

I enter the code to the flat, and she goes inside first.

"I'm craving something to eat. What do you think we—"

Her words catch in her throat as I pull her by the arm and slam her against the door. I grab both her wrists and shove them above her head.

She gasps, her green eyes filling with excitement so tangible, I can feel it over the black rage swirling in my brain.

"What were you doing back there, Green?"

"I don't know what you're talking about."

She's provoking me on purpose, and fuck if it isn't working. I yank her dress up, then my trousers and boxers down.

She bites her lower lip, her tits rising and falling heavily against my chest.

"You don't know, huh? Because it seemed to me you were allowing that fucker from accounting to flirt with you before I kicked him out."

"I was?" Her eyes widen with mock disbelief.

I lift her up by a hand under her thigh, and she doesn't need an invitation as her legs wrap around my waist.

"You'll pay for it, Green."

"I will?" she whispers in my ear.

I slam inside her so hard, my balls slap against her arse. Fucking fuck. She feels so right—so damn right.

She moans aloud as I fuck her hard and fast against the door. The bangs and the slaps of flesh against flesh echo in the silence.

Thankfully, for the neighbours' sake, the flat is soundproof.

Kim's groans fill the air and her mouth opens in that wordless 'O'.

"You like provoking me, Green? You like how I pulled you out in front of all of them, claiming you as mine?"

"Yes," she whimpers as I hit her sensitive spot over and over again until she's screaming my name.

I follow her soon after, the force of my release knocking us both cold. Her head falls against my shoulder and she stares up at me with that dreamy, utterly pleasured smile.

"I love it when you don't hold back, Xan."

The haziness of the orgasm slowly withers away as I recall the reason why this particular release felt good. It's because I haven't fucked her this hard in weeks.

"Oh, fuck." I carry her to the bedroom and lay her on the bed. Our cat, London, jumps away but remains at the door. I swear she's the biggest voyeur on this planet.

Kim bites the corner of her lip and still looks at me with those 'fuck me' eyes that keep luring me close.

I place a hand on the bump of her womb. "Is she okay?"

"She's fine." She pulls me over by the neck and removes my tie, then undoes my buttons. "You're awfully overdressed."

She doesn't stop until she removes my shirt and nuzzles her nose against her name that's tattooed on my heart. My wife loves that a bit too much.

My fingers lay in her hair that still has her signature green strands, although they're not as loud now. "The baby, Kim. What if I hurt her?"

"You didn't." She gives me a dirty look. "If you

hadn't started holding back, I wouldn't have provoked you today. Blame yourself."

"But I don't want to hurt our baby." It freaks me the fuck out that I could damage her if I keep my usual rough pace.

The doctor said it's fine, but it still makes me nervous as hell.

It doesn't help that my beautiful wife has become so hormonal since the pregnancy that she even interrupts me during work, lying on my desk and demanding pregnant woman care.

Since we both have crappy mothers that are thankfully out of our lives now, Kim has been nervous about the mum's role, but I know she'll be the best one alive.

She's been a mother figure to Kirian his entire life without even realising it. That's why he never asked about Jeanine when she left.

Now, he's excited about becoming an uncle and has begun threatening me to take care of his sister or he'll 'kick me'. Dad and Calvin have been calling daily and sending all sorts of shit since they learnt we're expecting.

For the past eight years I've spent with Kim, I've been the luckiest and happiest bastard alive.

There hasn't been a day where she doesn't make me laugh with her goofiness, or where she doesn't root for me to be the best version of myself. Just like I do for her.

That's what we've been doing all this time, being the best we could.

Kim has never stopped healing, but now, she looks back on that last year in RES with nostalgia. She doesn't hide her scars anymore. She could've had plastic surgery on her wrist, but she's chosen not to. Whenever someone asks her about it, she says it was a time when she was lost, and then she found me and I found her.

And after that, we were never lost again.

Kim kneels on the bed and runs her fingertips over my semi-hard cock. "If her mum is happy, she'll be happy."

"Is that so?"

"Totally." She grips me harder.

I groan. "You're killing me, Green."

"Admit it, you love it."

"Oh, I do." I take her scarred wrist with the bracelet dangling from it. She's never removed it since that day I put it back on her.

Just like the wedding ring. And no, I didn't marry her the following day of the proposal. I had to wait an entire month.

Small price to pay for finally having her by my side in all possible ways.

People marry their soulmates or those who complete them. I married the woman who gave meaning to my life.

She's not only my soulmate, my life wouldn't have existed without her.

"Make me yours, Xan."

"You already are, Green."

"Will you remind me again?"

"Oh, I will."

I flip her over and she squeals, then gasps as my lips claim hers.

NINETEEN

Ronan

Age Twenty-Four

So here's the thing. I told you before that being me is easy, and it is, in a way. You just have to skip the whole being inside your head shit.

Which I've mastered.

Like, no kidding. I'm the king of all that.

Do you know what my trick is? I choose to be inside my lovely wife's head instead. Which isn't hard. She lets me in willingly. And I don't just mean inside her pussy and arse and mouth. Those are an everyday pleasure—thank fuck for that.

Teal also lets me in on all her beautiful thoughts that no one but me has access to. Well, maybe me and Knox, but her twin brother doesn't count since he decided to relocate to the States for his new life there, and we barely see him in holidays.

So I'm the only one she's got—thank fuck for that, too.

Lars has started to become friends with her, but Lars doesn't count either because I can kick him out every day. And if you were wondering, yup, he does have a black book. I caught him writing in it the other day like a teenager with angst issues.

Anyway, where were we? Right. Me and Teal. The only two who matter, and if anyone tells you otherwise, then you shouldn't listen to them.

When we first got married a few years ago, I thought Teal would be the type of person who would need to hide at times. Not that I was going to let her, but that was her modus operandi when we were engaged. Colour me surprised when, instead of disappearing, she sought me out.

Sometimes, when it gets to be too much and she needs a place to hide, my embrace is that place. When she needs a screaming outlet, I take her to the mountains and let her go at it, because that's how she deals with the past.

Over the years, those times have eventually disappeared. Ever since we graduated from university, she's been even more focused about our future. She's been learning from Ethan. And Agnus—the fucker whom I'm not killing, because murder is unfortunately still frowned upon.

I've also been trying to learn about the family affairs from Dad, and let's just say that Lord Edric Astor is strict as fuck when it comes to business. I normally have Lars stand with me as some sort of an ally, but when dealing with my dad, that bastard is usually Team Earl Astor. I contemplated bitching to Mum about it, but that would label me as a mama's boy, and I'm totally not—a mama's boy, I mean. I'm married, thank you very much.

Despite Dad's strict rules that come somewhere from medieval times, I know that he wants what's best for me. Over the past few years since the one who shall not be named died, Dad apologised to me for not seeing what happened sooner. He even hugged me. No fucking kidding. My father, Earl Edric Astor, the successor of the Astor family name, almost lost his diploma from his ancestors when he showed some emotion and actually hugged his only son.

It was just that once, but it felt like both of us needed that closure. Since then, we've been building back our father-son relationship that I thought was long dead.

Turns out, no. It's long from dead, and Dad's new purpose in life seems to be torturing me. Sorry, I mean, *teaching* me business the right, strict way.

"Does that mean I'm not supposed to invite everyone to the company like it's a party?" I asked him once, just to be a dick.

He stared me down with that condescending gaze of his. "Are you joking or should I search for another heir?"

"Joking, joking. Jeez." I pointed at myself. "How could you even think about exchanging this eternal sunshine with someone else?"

His lips twitched in a smile, which meant he

thought I was funny. "Hear that, Lars? He called himself eternal sunshine."

"Yes, your lordship." Lars judged me with his
snobby expression. "I will witness in your favour."

"Lars! You fucking traitor."

"You got yourself into this, young lord. Don't
blame it on me."

Let's just say that those sessions happen more often
than I like to admit. And yeah, I had my revenge by
spiking Lars's original tea with cheap stuff from the
store. He found out about it, though, and I'm pretty
sure his black book came in handy during his ranting
sessions.

At the end of the day, it doesn't matter what he
writes about me, because everyone knows I'm the heart
of this house. Whenever Teal and I come for dinner,
like today, everyone at the table waits for my jokes—
especially my mum and my wife. They're my number
one supporters, thank you very much.

Teal retreated to my old room in my parents' house
to rest while I had a small meeting with Dad in his
home office.

I'm about ready to take her home and fuck her
until tomorrow. She spent the entire day with the other
girls, Elsa, Kim, Silver and Astrid, while I had to listen
to Lars bitching at me to 'pay attention'. Then we had
dinner here.

It's been exactly eighteen hours since I last touched
her.

The platonic skin-to-skin doesn't count. And

whenever I slipped my hand under the dinner table to tease her, she pushed it away.

Teal might appear like a rebel, but she respects my parents too much. I'm trying to make touching her under the table a normal occurrence. I'll let you know how it goes.

Once I'm finally done with the boring meeting at Dad's office, I practically jog down the hall towards my old room.

I find Teal sleeping on her side, her petite frame barely taking up any space on the bed. I slowly close the door, trying not to make a sound, and kick my shoes away.

I slip in behind her, the mattress dipping with my weight. Then I sneak one hand under her arm until I grab her breast. She moans softly as she snuggles back into me.

"Wake up, *belle*, I miss you."

"Mmm."

"I will speak French to you, *mon petit coeur adoré*."

She opens one of her eyes, peeking up at me. "You will?"

I grin, knowing exactly which buttons to push. "I will only speak French if that's your kink."

"Nah, that's not my kink." She cups my cheek. "You are."

"Holy fuck. Repeat that."

"You're my kink, Ronan. You always have been."

"And I always will be." I flip her so that she's underneath me. "Now, let me satisfy your kink."

"Wait."

"Nope. I can't wait until we're home. I'm hungry."

"You just ate."

"I didn't eat you."

She laughs, but she still places a hand on my chest, stopping me. "I have something to tell you."

"After dinner. My main course, I mean, not whatever we had in the dining room."

She chuckles, her happiness filling the space. I can't get enough of the sound of her laughter, of how easily I can bring that out of her. It's like I appear and she automatically smiles. I say anything and she looks at me as if I'm the wisest person alive. I'm not. But the fact that she looks at me that way, even after so many years, makes me the luckiest fucker on this planet.

I grab her by the waist. "Remove your hand, *ma belle*. Don't leave me starving."

"Ronan..."

"*Oui, ma puce?*"

"I think I'm pregnant."

I stop with my hand on her jeans' buttons. "You're...what?"

"I took two tests and they said positive, but it could be false, like Silver back in school, you know? I'll have to take another one and go to the doctor, but...yeah, I think I'm pregnant."

"Whoa."

"Is that a good whoa or a bad one?" She's watching me so intently, unblinking, as if afraid she'll miss something if she does.

"A fucking bewildered one. You're carrying a baby."

"*Your* baby."

"My baby," I repeat, a weird sense of pride hitting me out of nowhere. I mean, we knew we would have children one day, but since Teal admitted to the therapist that she's afraid of the idea of becoming a mother, I thought we could wait like Xan and Kim, or Cole and Silver, who still haven't even gotten married.

I have no doubt that Teal will kick arse as a mother. It's not that she doesn't care, it's that she's selective when it comes to the ones she cares about, and I'm positive that our child will make the top of that list. After me, of course.

"Didn't you say we should wait?" I ask. "Are you okay with it?"

She nods frantically. "I can't wait when it comes to you, Ronan. You make me want to burn every obstacle in the way as long as you're by my side."

"That's because you're smart as fuck, *ma belle*. You know what's up."

She laughs, her dark eyes sparkling.

I place my hand on her stomach. "So our offspring is in here?"

"Yes. If he or she is anything like you, we're going to have our hands full."

"Hey! I was a good boy. Ask Lars. Actually, no, I gave him hell whenever he made me drink milk. Ask Mum. She'll tell you how much of a good boy I was."

"You mean, I should ask the same Charlotte who's always on your side, no matter what you do?"

"I'm her miracle, love. She has to be on my side. That's how it works."

"You're unbelievable."

"Not more than this." I keep touching her stomach, trying to find something, anything. "Are you sure there's a living being here?"

"Yeah, it just doesn't show now."

"Shit. Does this mean I shouldn't have fucked you yesterday?"

"Elsa mentioned that the doctor said it was fine."

"Thank fuck for that." I grin. "Because I'm in the mood to celebrate."

TWENTY

Cole

Age Twenty-Eight

It might be ten years overdue, but Aiden finally got punched again. I didn't do it in front of our wives, because they tend to be soft and have zero tolerance for violence.

While I don't prefer it either, I wasn't going to sit still after I learnt about the actual truth of what happened ten years ago.

Aiden staggers to his feet, clutching his nose—that I think is broken, by the way. "What the fuck was that for?"

My fists are still clenched at my sides as I stare him down. We're at his office after a business meeting with both Jonathan King and Ethan Steel. I was biding my time until they left before I punched him. I figured his father and his father-in-law wouldn't stand for it while I beat him to a pulp.

Not even the meeting could've cooled me down. Ever since I accidentally heard Elsa apologise to Silver, I couldn't stay still.

"I didn't know you thought you were pregnant back then." Elsa's face paled as she held Silver by the shoulders, her fingers trembling. "Oh my God, I feel so terrible for hitting you. It's not just about the pregnancy. I don't even know what came over me at the time. I overreacted, and I'm so sorry. I'm really, *really* sorry, Silver."

My wife laughed and rubbed her arm. "I've already forgotten about it. You didn't know. Not like the arsehole Aiden."

"Aiden knew?" Elsa shrieked and Silver had to shush her, then take her away.

Aiden knew.

He knew that Silver thought she was pregnant and didn't stop Elsa until after. He didn't even tell me, knowing I would have stopped Elsa myself.

This selfish bastard knew and did nothing about it.

I've always had regrets about that part. It didn't matter that she wasn't pregnant. The fact that she was hurt still sits wrong with me. Even if she provoked me before it happened.

Aiden wipes blood from the corner of his mouth. "You fucking bastard. Are you jealous of my face, is that it?"

"You *knew*." My voice is calm, despite the utter chaos I'm planning for this fucker.

"That you're a petty little bitch? Sure."

"You knew she thought she was pregnant. She confided in you and you let her get beaten."

He seems to grasp on to what I'm talking about since he pauses wiping his mouth and scoffs. "Confided in me? More like she threatened me."

"You still knew."

"Chill, arsehole. She wasn't pregnant."

I grab him by the collar of his shirt and stare straight into his soulless eyes. "That's not the part that matters. You knew and didn't protect her."

"Not that it makes a difference, but I did."

"You did, how? By letting Elsa punch her?"

"By stopping Elsa. I had flashbacks from when her mother used to do that shit. So yeah, maybe I didn't do it fast enough, but I did it, and if I hadn't made her leave, I have no clue what Elsa would've done or if I could've stopped her. She wasn't herself back then, and you know how Queens doesn't give up. Besides, why the fuck are you acting high and mighty when you watched her with a bloody smile on your face?" He pushes me away and I release him with a shove.

"I didn't know."

"Right, and that magically makes it okay."

"Shut the fuck up, Aiden, before I break your nose for real."

His face remains blank as he flips me off. "Hit me again and I'll ruin your features. I doubt Queens would stay with you then. After all, your looks are the only thing working in your favour."

I resist the urge to ram his face into the sofa before I leave the office. I'm still agitated during the drive home, and it takes everything in me not to go back and empty my grudge into that fucker.

It doesn't matter that we've been sort of friends for the majority of our lives. He still pisses me off the most.

And yes, I'm still not over the fact that he was Silver's fiancé first or that he had her first fucking waltz.

By the time I reach home, I have to stop at the threshold to calm my breathing. No matter how chaotic things get, I don't like bringing that to Silver. It took us so long to finally get married, and even though it's been a few months since we tied the knot, it feels like only days.

I can't get enough of the reality that my Butterfly is now my wife, my world, and nothing—and no one—will ever change that.

The thought of her puts a smile on my face. I step into the bedroom, removing my jacket and tie on the way, but there's no trace of her.

I place my clothes on the chair, and I'm about to head to the piano room, where she spends some of her time, when my feet come to a halt at the sound of heaving coming from the bathroom. I barge inside, grabbing towels on the way.

Sure enough, Silver is kneeling in front of the toilet, emptying her stomach.

I rub soothing circles on her back while holding her blonde hair off her neck so it doesn't bother her.

"What's wrong?" I continue stroking her back. "Did you eat something bad?"

She shakes her head without looking at me.

"Then what is it, Silver? Let me take you to the doctor so…" I trail off when she stares up at me, smiling, as tears shine in her eyes.

"I'm pregnant, Cole."

"You're…what?"

She reaches inside her bag on the floor and rummages through it. "I thought it was a false alarm at first and didn't believe the tests. I know I should've waited for you to go to the doctor, but I got so excited and I didn't want to disappoint you too in case it wasn't real. The next thing I know, I made an appointment and…" she retrieves a sonogram. "I am pregnant, Cole. It's true this time."

She places the sonogram in my palm and I stare at the little life pictured there. The baby that Silver has dreamt about since that day ten years ago when we found out it was a false positive.

And because she yearned for it, I wanted it with my whole heart, too. Anything that Silver wants automatically becomes my dream.

"You're pregnant," I repeat, staring between her and the sonogram.

She grabs my hand and places it on her stomach. "Our baby is right here, Cole."

I stroke her hair away from her face, unveiling

her ecstatic expression, despite the tired look in her eyes and paleness of her skin.

"It's finally here."

"It is." She kisses my cheek softly before pulling back. "Thank you for giving me this."

"'Thank you for being mine, Butterfly."

She stands on wobbly feet, hugging me, and I tighten my hold around her as she whispers against my chest, "Always."

PART FIVE

The Group

TWENTY-ONE

Astrid

Age Thirty-One

I never realised just how vibrant Levi's group of friends was until we started meeting for dinners like this one.

The Meet Up has become too small for everyone and their kids. Our twin boys, Brandon and Landon, are playing with their cousin Eli, Remington, who's Teal and Ronan's boy. Cole and Silver's daughter, Ava, is barely walking as she holds on to Cecily, Kim and Xander's daughter.

Our third baby, Glyndon, is with her grandparents. She's thoroughly a Grandpa's little girl—from both Jonathan's and Dad's sides. Like, she barely leaves them and she's the only one Jonathan doesn't mind when Aurora brings her over.

Levi is playing chess against Aiden, and Cole is helping my husband cheat because he's in for anything that includes bringing Aiden down.

Elsa, Silver, and I are preparing the drinks while Teal

and Kim are trying to ward off their husbands from stealing all the food.

Nothing ever changes. The horsemen are all still playful in one way or another. They merely grew up and with that, they've become more ruthless about what they want.

Levi quit football as of the last season, while he was at the peak of his career. He's now leading King Enterprise with Aiden.

Jonathan, although now in his mid-fifties, is not letting them have full control. However, he's slowly loosening his iron grip with each accomplishment Aiden and Levi bring to the table.

And in a way, I think his complete devotion to his wife is what's making him pull back a little in favour of the younger generation.

Jonathan will always be Jonathan with his controlling nature and scary wrath, but ever since Aurora came into his life, he's turned a new page, especially with Aiden and Levi. Now, it feels as if they both respect him, despite how they disliked and clashed with him in the past.

That's why Elsa and I thank Aurora every chance we get. She tamed the lion, and we will forever be grateful for that.

I'm proud of how far Levi has come. He went after his football dream, and when he knew that his career wouldn't last much longer, he switched back to the family business. It wasn't because of Jonathan's extortion—although he did make him study business at the same time as playing football at the beginning.

Over the years, my husband has been growing into this focused person whose only care is his family. He loves me and the children beyond words. We're constantly at the forefront of his mind in anything he does.

When I have an upcoming exhibition, he sometimes spends the entire day with the children outside so I can focus. And if they happen to stay in the house, he teaches them that their mummy needs to concentrate so she can make masterpieces. When Landon asked him what's a masterpiece, Levi told him it's something like him, his brother, and his sister.

He can be over the top sometimes, but in the best way possible. He's my number one supporter and that says something since both Dad and the bug, Daniel, fight to buy my paintings even when I tell them not to.

"So I'm curious about something," Elsa tells Silver, pulling her attention away from whatever conversation she's having with Cole through their eyes alone.

"What?" Silver places the cups on the tray.

"Don't take it the wrong way, okay?"

"Of course." Silver's brow furrows, as does mine because they've been friends since university. Everyone knows they threw the past behind them and moved on.

"It's just that I've been curious about this for so long." Elsa runs her nails over a bottle of beer.

"About what?"

"Remember that time at school when you posted a selfie of you by Aiden's pool? There was a hand at the bottom of the picture."

Silver's lips pull in a shy smile. "Oh, that."

"Aiden told me it wasn't him and I believe him. But who was it?"

"Who do you think?" Silver motions at her husband, who's now holding little Ava on his lap as she claps joyfully at the chess game.

"What was Cole doing in Aiden's pool?" Elsa asks.

"He followed me. It was around the time when I used my engagement with Aiden to make him jealous. As soon as I got there, Cole showed up and kind of kicked Aiden out of his own pool."

"He did that?" I ask with a laugh.

"Yeah, Cole can be crazy sometimes."

Elsa raises a brow. "You mean when it comes to you."

Silver touches her butterfly necklace, smiling. "Yeah. I guess so."

"You guess so?" Elsa and I say in unison, teasing her.

"Stop it." She wiggles free. "It's not like Aiden or Levi are any different."

"True that." Elsa grins. "The other day, Eli walked in on us while...you know, and because he was interrupted, Aiden sat him down and told him there's no more sneaking into the third floor or Daddy is going to be very mad."

"At least Aiden was diplomatic about it." I chuckle. "Levi actually yelled at Brandon to get the fuck out. He lost his dad of the year award that night."

"Thankfully, Ava sleeps soundly at night." Silver shakes her head. "She wakes up early and makes it her mission to wake us, though. Having a toddler is no joke."

The three of us sigh in agreement before we burst into laughter.

Levi raises his head from the game, and as usual, time stops when I get lost in his blue-grey eyes. They're like a magnet to a secret part of me.

He motions upstairs with a slight tilt of his head, and I try to reprimand him, but he just smirks and keeps tilting his head, then motions at Brandon and Landon.

I love those two to death, but because of them and their little sister, we barely get time for us. Our only reprieves are either when Jonathan and Aurora take them or in settings like these where they're busy playing with the other kids.

So I tell the girls I'll be back and precede Levi upstairs.

TWENTY-TWO

Aiden

Age Thirty

Levi follows Astrid upstairs and I shake my head, pretending to focus on the chess game my cousin purposefully lost so he could piss off.

Cole settles opposite me and gives his baby girl the queen piece. She watches it with awe, almost like that first time Jonathan sat me beside him and taught me the art of chess. That's actually one of the few calm father-son moments I remember with him.

Small hands pull on my trousers and I stare down at my nephew. "Where's Mummy, Uncle?"

I grab Landon and sit him on my lap. "Making other babies."

His blue-green eyes double in size. "Other babies?"

"Yeah." I pat his back. "Hang in there, buddy. It'll be wild."

Cole shakes his head at me. "Stop terrorising the boy."

I flip him off behind Landon's back. Ava sees me, though, and although I think she doesn't understand the gesture, she giggles. I wink at her and she laughs more.

Landon points a finger in her direction. "Other babies like her, Uncle?"

"Exactly."

"I like Ava." He grins.

"You don't." Eli appears by my other side and before I can help him, he climbs up on my other thigh. He's older than Landon, and bigger, too, so he doesn't even sit on anyone's lap anymore. However, he becomes clingy when other children are around. I swear it's Ronan's loathsome influence. He's teaching them all his clingy nature.

"Yes, I do." Landon pokes a finger at him.

Eli pokes him back. "You do *not*. You said she was annoying."

"You did, you liar."

Eli twists his lips but remains silent, then pulls on my shirt. "Daddy."

"What?" I lean over so he can whisper.

"Make him go away."

"Lan?"

"Yeah."

"Why?"

"I don't like him here."

I smile to myself, shaking my head. Eli's passive-aggressive game is strong, even though he's little.

It might have something to do with the fact that he's an only child.

He stopped asking for other siblings once I sat him down and told him that his mum can't get pregnant again due to her heart condition. The doctor said we could try and see how it will go, but I'm completely against that idea.

It was already a miracle that we got Eli, and we're not going to be greedy about it. Elsa asked me the other day if Eli's enough for me.

He's more than enough. He's the only kid we'll ever need. Even if he wasn't enough, I would never risk her life for a non-existent one. Her health comes first and everything else is secondary.

She complains that I'm too strict and overbearing when it comes to her medical appointments and medicine, but that's because the thought of something happening to her terrifies the fuck out of me.

I've had her for twelve years. We've been married for eleven, and sometimes, I wake up and think I'm back to the time where I thought I'd lost her in that basement.

Sometimes, I wake up with images of blood marring her chest and hair and her unmoving body in my brain.

That memory will haunt me for life. The fact that I lost her after I escaped that wretched basement still aches more than I like to admit.

So, yes, I guess I have the right to be as overbearing as it can get because her well-being comes before anything else.

Speaking of the beautiful angel, she carries the drinks towards us and places them beside the chessboard. Landon hops down to snatch a cola.

Elsa stands on Eli's side and strokes his hair back. When she speaks to him, her voice is soft, welcoming, like she's singing him a lullaby. "What do you want, hon?"

"Nothing."

"Is it not here? Do you want something else from the kitchen?"

"He can get it himself." I pull her so she's by my side, and no, I'm not jealous of my own son. It's that she's too doting on him and that will turn him into a mama's boy like Ronan, and that's not something I'll allow. I push him down my leg. "Off you go."

He glares at Landon one more time before he stalks in Brandon's direction. "I'll have juice, Mummy."

She starts to follow him, but I hold her by the waist, my head touching her dress.

"Aiden…" When she attempts to struggle, it only makes me tighten my hold on her.

"He can take care of himself." I pause. "Actually, I'm pretty sure Jonathan and Aurora miss him, so he should spend the weekend there."

"Stop shipping our son off any chance you get."

I graze my teeth against her side, and even though I'm separated from her skin by cloth, she shudders as I murmur, "No."

She stares down at me with raw lust that makes my dick rock-fucking-hard. I'll never get over the way she looks at me, the way her blue eyes brighten and the way she speaks without words, telling me to take her, to own her. To make her all mine.

It doesn't matter how long we've been together. It doesn't matter that she sleeps in my arms every night and wakes up wrapped all around me.

Even as an old man, I will never get enough of this woman. I will never get enough of the brightness she brings to my life. She's the calm to my storm. The light to my darkness. And I don't take any of that for granted. I worship her every day so she knows how fucking grateful I am for finding her again.

For having her.

For breathing her in every night.

For seeing her face every morning.

"The rooms are upstairs." Cole's bored voice interrupts our connection.

"And the door is just there." I point at it with my middle finger.

Elsa blushes before she slips from underneath my touch and picks up Ava, who's struggling to reach the floor.

"That's not true!" Ronan pushes Xan away as the two of them, their wives, and Silver join us.

"Now what?" Cole tugs on Silver's hand so she falls on to his lap. The fucking hypocrite was just pointing out the rooms for me.

"Xan here was saying that he's Kimmy's first and last when I actually dated her first."

"No, you didn't." Xander elbows him.

"*Mais oui.* Remember that date at Mum's favourite restaurant, Kimmy?"

"Your mum's favourite restaurant, huh?" Teal crosses her arms, staring her husband down, even though he's way taller than her.

He quickly backpedals, holding her hands. "You know that's not what I meant, *ma belle.* Xan was a dick at the time—more than usual, I mean—and I was only being my usual Prince Charming self. It's not me, it's my genes."

"Shut it, Ron." Xander elbows him again and gathers Cecily off the floor. She snuggles in his embrace, ignoring everyone else. Xander feels smug whenever we tell him she's a daddy's girl.

"Hey, Remi," Ronan calls out for his son and he comes running, jumping in his father's arms. "Tell your mummy who loves her most in the world."

"Daddy and Remi."

"That's right." Ronan fist-bumps with him.

"And Uncle Knox!"

"And your Uncle Knox, when he's not getting himself in trouble."

"My brother doesn't get himself in trouble." Teal goes straight to the defensive.

"He kind of does," my wife says. "Though it's not always his fault."

"Thank you!" Teal squeezes Elsa's shoulder.

"You did well and will be rewarded by Lars later." Ronan puts his son to his feet. "Off you go, my second in command."

Remi stands upright and makes a salute. "Yes, sir."

Everyone laughs as he runs at full speed and crashes into Brandon and Eli.

Everyone except me, because I'm contemplating a way to kidnap Elsa out of here and have her all to myself.

After Eli falls asleep.

I pull out my phone and email Jonathan because he dislikes texts. Usually, I would purposely text him, but I need him for grandpa duties this weekend.

It's been some time since I had Jonathan's island all for me and my wife.

From: Aiden King
To: Jonathan King
Subject: Don't You Miss Your Grandkid?
I'll bring him over this weekend.

From: Jonathan King
To: Aiden King
Subject: Don't You Miss Your Grandkid?
No.

He's probably planning to go to the island with my stepmum himself, and he can get stiff as fuck when it comes to her time. I smirk as I type.

From: Aiden King
To: Jonathan King
Subject: Don't You Miss Your Grandkid?

You had your chance. I'm calling Aurora.
From: Jonathan King
To: Aiden King
Subject: Don't You Miss Your Grandkid?
Don't.

I pull Aurora's number and text her.

Aiden: Elsa needs time to decompress. Can you have Eli this weekend?

Her reply is immediate.

Aurora: Absolutely! I miss his face.

My smirk widens as I pull back the exchange with my father.

From: Aiden King
To: Jonathan King
Subject: Don't You Miss Your Grandkid?
Already done.

"What are you plotting?" a soft voice whispers from my right as I tuck the phone in my pocket.

Elsa stares at me with slightly narrowed eyes, as if she knows exactly what I've done.

"Just some negotiations with Jonathan."

She raises a brow. "Just Jonathan?"

"I might have deferred to Aurora."

"Aiden!" She clutches me by the shoulder. "Stop using her against your father."

"I'm not using her. It's mutually beneficial. It's not my problem that Jonathan doesn't see it that way."

She chuckles under her breath. "You're awful."

"But you still love me?"

Her lips brush against my cheek as she whispers, "When did I ever stop?"

"I never stopped loving you since that day I first saw you when we were just kids, sweetheart."

TWENTY-THREE

Kimberley

I tug on Xander's bicep. "Let Cecily go so she can play with the other kids."

"You mean so they'll hurt her?" He tickles her tummy. "Not that I would let anyone hurt my little Cecily."

She breaks out in giggles, dimples creasing her cheeks as she holds on to him with all her might. "Daddy!"

I shake my head as I take her from his arms and put her to her feet. She staggers for a bit before she breaks into a run towards the others. He's making her so spoilt, it's on a whole different level.

"Why did you do that?" He frowns, following her with his gaze as she stands beside Remi, holding on to him as she did to her daddy.

I smooth a crease in his shirt on his shoulder, and yeah, it could be just an excuse to touch him. Truth is, I can't stop touching Xander. So what if we've been married for nine years? When in his presence, I feel like the little girl who snuck into his house to sleep beside him.

"You, Kir, Dad, and Lewis are turning her into a spoilt little princess."

"Which she should be." He grins, showing his own dimples as he palms my cheeks. "You don't have to be jealous, Green. If you want attention, all you have to do is ask. Actually, scratch that. I would give you attention without you having to ask."

His lips meet mine and I pull back before he deepens the kiss in front of everyone. "That's not what I meant."

"Yeah, right."

"You'll come back to my words one day and by then, it will be too late."

"It will never be too late, because Cecily won't leave my side. Kir agrees, by the way."

I sigh, thinking of my baby brother. Although he's twenty and at university now, so he's not exactly a baby anymore.

Xan's lips brush against my temple. "You miss him?"

A small period of silence is all he needs to know there's something up. Xan is the one person on this planet who can read me better than anyone. Just like I have the ability to read him.

Leaning my head on his shoulder, I sigh. "I do. Do you think he'll kick me out if I go visit?"

"You saw him last weekend, Green. And you say I'm spoiling Cecily? Look at you with Kir."

"I worry."

"He's a grown man. Leave him be."

"Fine. I will go to visit next weekend, I guess."

He laughs. "You're so fucking adorable."

I wrap my arms around him as we re-join our circle of friends. We've come so far in the twelve years since we left Royal Elite School.

My demons are in the past, and although the scars have never disappeared, they've faded away and I can now breathe properly. Sometimes, I wonder what would've happened if I'd stayed in that black hole. Other times, I completely forget about the what-ifs and remain in the present.

I wouldn't have gotten this far without the man holding on to me as if I'm his world.

I followed my dream and became a sociologist who's able to help kids who are like I once was. Kids who've been mentally or physically abused. Kids who need help but don't know how to ask for it.

That's my best accomplishment in life, aside from the spoilt little princess Cecily and the hunk of a husband who turns my nights into the wildest rollercoaster rides.

Xander and Ronan formed some sort of a partnership just like Aiden, Levi, and Cole. Teal and Silver also followed in their husbands' footsteps and chose business.

Elsa is an architect, who's more focused on her aunt and uncle's engineering firm instead of her father's corporation. Astrid has been slowly turning into a renowned artist that we're all proud to say we know on a personal level.

All of us have come a long way, but at moments like this, it feels like time can stop. Like we can be forever young.

My eyes meet Silver's as she sits on Cole's lap, and we both smile in a knowing way. If she tells him what she told me earlier, then Cole will be a happy man tonight—more than usual, I mean.

It's crazy to think that Silver and I were enemies back in school. Now, she's my best friend again, along with Elsa.

It took me some time to get past how she used to treat me, but after hearing her reasons and her apology, I couldn't hold a grudge against her. Xan says I forgive easily and he's lucky for that; however, the truth is, I don't like holding on to the bad. That shit festers inside and destroys you.

Besides, Silver and I have always had a bond since we were little girls. We just built on that and picked up where we left off. Sort of like Xan and I.

My heart ached when I heard about what she's been through, from the pressure to the pregnancy's false alarm to the stalker.

She's the type who buries everything inside and tries to take care of everyone from afar, even if it makes her appear in a negative light.

Now that we're back in each other's lives, we've built a bond that I never thought would be possible in a million years.

"I'll go with you." Xan's words and his kiss on the top of my head bring me back from my reverie.

"Go with me where?"

"To Kir. You're still thinking about him, aren't you? And if he complains to you about how often you visit, I'll punch him."

"Hey, don't punch my baby brother."

"I'll punch anyone who hurts you. Kir included."

"He's your half-brother, too," I whisper.

"That doesn't give him a pass."

I chuckle, leaning my head against his chest. "You're impossible."

"For you, Green. Only you."

Only me.

I can die a happy woman right here and now.

TWENTY-FOUR

Teal

The four of us leave the kids with their fathers as we sit around for a drink.

Astrid and Levi are still absent, so it's just Elsa, Kim, Silver, and me.

Aiden has both Landon and Brandon on his lap. Eli refuses to join since he's a 'big boy'.

Cecily holds on to her father as if her life depends on it. Little Ava keeps playing with Cole's tie and giggling whenever he tickles her.

Remi is casually draped over Ronan's shoulder. I swear, those two have the most chill father-son relationship ever. It's like they're friends, which isn't so hard to believe considering that Ronan is forever young. It doesn't matter how old he gets, he's still the life of every gathering, and right now, he's plotting a game to keep the children busy. There's a reason why Ronan is every child's favourite uncle.

Our Remi is so cool about it, too. I thought he would be jealous that other kids would be taking up his father's time, but he said, "No, Mummy. That means Daddy is da best."

It's like he's his wingman.

My heart always flutters when I see them together. My two men. Who knew there would be a day when I would be a wife and a mother, and not only that, but also have the best family out there.

I have a husband who wakes me up on a daily basis with his head buried between my legs to 'relax me' and a son who's learning from his father to bring me breakfast in bed.

For someone who hardly had a family, having Ronan and Remi feels like an eternal dream.

One I don't ever want to wake up from.

"Stop it." Silver's voice brings me to the present.

She's elbowing Kim, who keeps laughing under her breath while Silver is blushing.

"What's going on?" Elsa asks.

"Nothing." Kim hides her laughter again.

"She was teasing me." Silver narrows her eyes on her childhood friend.

"I was only telling the truth about how Cole sat you on his lap earlier."

"Yeah, right. As if Xan doesn't do the same." Silver nudges her playfully and they both break out in laughter.

"You guys are lucky you've known your husbands since you were young." Elsa sighs, taking a sip of her martini.

"You met Aiden when you were young, too," Kim says.

"Yeah, but I didn't live with him like you guys did."

"You're lucky you didn't." Silver sighs. "He was a wanker from a young age. Cole, too. Kim is the only actual lucky one here because Xan was like a ring on her finger since they were in nappies."

Kim's face flushes. "That's not true."

"Yes, it is. He always stood up for you and even beat Cole and Aiden whenever they bothered you."

"Well, I guess."

"You guess?" Silver attacks Kim's ticklish side until they both break down in giggles.

"Rub it in, would you?" Elsa tears her gaze from them and focuses on me. "How about you, Teal? Don't you wish you'd met Ronan when he was young?"

"No. Not really. I believe we met at the right time. Any earlier and it would've been off, you know?" My gaze automatically finds his and he winks. I smile back, feeling all sorts of fireworks explode in my chest.

I want him for myself.

As much as I love getting together with the girls and seeing all the kids play with each other, I'm actually selfish about my Ron, and even Remi.

I want my husband's time for myself. I want to sleep in his arms and have him speak French to me.

I guess it's time to go home.

TWENTY-FIVE

Silver

"**C**all me afterwards, okay?" Kim squeezes me in a hug.

"I will." I kiss her cheek. "Give that to Cecily on my behalf."

"You say that as if she spends time with me when her daddy is around."

I smile as I wave at her, then at Teal and Ronan, who are pulling out of the Meet Up.

Aiden left with Elsa, Eli, and Astrid's twin boys because their parents are still MIA.

Cole straps a sleeping Ava in the baby seat in the back of the car and kisses her adorable cheek.

"Daddy…" she mumbles in her sleep. "Mummy…"

A smile grazes my lips as Cole kisses her forehead before he joins me. I throw a fleeting glance at my messages, then place my phone in my bag.

After putting his seatbelt on, Cole checks mine.

It's become a habit of his. The protectiveness of this man knows no limits. I'm addicted to it, in a way, and I can't imagine my life without his over-the-top protectiveness. Whenever we're with him, I completely let go because I know my baby girl and I are completely safe in his company.

He places a hand on my thigh—as usual—while he pulls the car out of the Meet Up.

For a moment in time, I'm lost watching his side profile and the way he's grown into this absolutely mouth-watering man. Not that he's ever been young. Cole has been an adult since he was a child. But he's currently rocking his thirties like no one else. His physique has kept its lean quality, yet he exudes a lethal type of calm that can be seen from the deep green of his eyes.

Just seeing him puts me in a constant mood to fuck or touch or anything that includes his skin on mine. Not that Cole lets me wait. He's normally the one who starts it. Like right now.

His fingers keep creeping beneath my dress, and my legs part of their own volition under his ministrations.

"Mum texted," I say casually, pretending that he's not about to finger me to an orgasm.

"She did?" he says in his usual calm tone, even as he inches his fingers up.

"She and Papa want to have Ava for the weekend."

"Tell them no one is taking my daughter away."

"They're not taking her away. She is their grandkid."

"And we're her parents, Butterfly. We waited for her more than they did."

That's true. Still, he's so possessive of her that Papa

and Mum barely have her overnight. They're older now and 'need their grandkid', as Mum keeps reminding me.

"You're hot." Cole rips his gaze from the road for a fraction of a second to focus on me.

"I know that." I still blush. We might have been married for two years and fully public for way longer than that, but Cole still manages to bring the little girl out from inside me. The girl who spied on him when he wasn't looking.

The girl who watched him while he watched everything else, and was oblivious when he watched her.

"No." He removes his hand from between my legs and places it on my forehead. "You're feverish. Did you have something to drink?"

"No."

"Then what is it?"

"I…let's go home first."

"Tell me, Silver."

"I have an entire evening planned."

He narrows his eyes on me. "An entire evening for what?"

A wave of nausea hits me out of the blue and I grab my mouth. "Stop the car."

He does and I open the door, flying out and heaving on the side of the road.

Cole joins me in a second, holding my hair and stroking my back. This scene is so similar to the other time.

"Silver…" Cole holds my shoulders after I finish. "Are you…"

Damn it. I really planned an evening for this, and

I even made Kim help me pick the candles and everything, but now, I don't have a choice.

I take his hand and place it on my stomach, nodding.

"You're pregnant?" he asks, eyes widening in wonder.

"I am. I found out this morning and planned a romantic night to celebrate. Now it's all ruined."

"Who says it's ruined?" He holds me to him, kissing my nose. "We'll celebrate until the morning if that's what you want. Thank you for being mine, Butterfly."

"Cole…"

He wipes my tears away with a smile and I groan, "Stupid hormones. They're going to make our lives hell now, like when we were expecting Ava."

"I couldn't give two fucks about that. As long as you're healthy, I'll take care of the hormones."

I bite my lower lip. "You will?"

"Oh, I fucking will." He carries me in his arms bridal style and I squeal, then laugh as he takes me to the car.

Cole doesn't wait until we get home.

TWENTY-SIX

The Men's Group Chat

Ronan: Emergency.

Ronan: I said, emergency, fuckers.

Cole: Now what? You put juice in your kid's milk again?

Xander: Or you messed up Teal's workspace and she's coming after your arse with an axe?

Aiden: Remi needs to get older so he can film that shit and send it over.

Ronan: *Premièrement*, my Remi would never betray me. *Deuxièmenent,* fuck you all. *Finalement,* it's none of your previous nonsense. I don't know what to get Teal for our anniversary. I took her everywhere and she doesn't like material shit. Give me inspiration.

Xander: Last anniversary, I bought Green a piece of land on which she can build a new children's centre. Best decision ever. And best sex ever that night.

Ronan: Teal has no use for a piece of land. Dammit.

Aiden: Buy her jewellery. Something she can have on all the time.

Ronan: She doesn't like jewellery. How about you, Cole? What did you get Silver on your last anniversary?

Cole: Pretty sure a baby.

Xander: *laughing out loud emoji*

Aiden: Are you knocking her up for sport, Nash?

Cole: You of all people should shut the fuck up, King.

Aiden: She was my fiancée first.

Cole: Just like Ron was Elsa's fiancé first and Xan was her boyfriend.

Xander: #Burn.

Ronan: Hey, fuckers. Me. Pay attention to *me*. I'm the one who called this up. Where's Levi anyway?

Levi: Over here. Don't care.

Xander: Have you thought about asking Knox? He should know what his sister would want.

Ronan: Jackpot! You're promoted to being my

best friend, Xan. I'll hang the award in your office tomorrow.

Xander: No thanks.

One day later…

Cole: How did it go, Ron?

Xander: He's been MIA for an entire day. Do you think he's dead? Should we file a missing person report?

Aiden: Damn. There should have been someone who filmed the whole murder scene.

Ronan: I'm here. I'm not dead, but you all will be next time I see you. And no, there was no murder scene.

Xander: So? What happened? Since when do you like suspense?

Ronan: I can't hear you over the halo clouding my head. Piss off.

Cole: I guess that means it went well?

Ronan: Well? Try fantastic. Try…adventurous.

Aiden: A threesome?

Ronan: Fuck you, King. I wouldn't share my Teal, even if I was offered the world.

Cole: La Débauche?

Ronan: Ding, ding, ding. One word, fuckers. You need lightening years to reach my level.

Ronan: Time for round two.

Aiden: How do you know if your wife is cheating on you?

Cole: Easy. You don't know.

Xander: Elsa is cheating on you?

Ronan: Hold my fucking beer. This shit is interesting. Is it me? Did she say my name while asleep? I knew she couldn't have possibly gotten over me.

Xander: And me. I know I should be sorry, but I'm kind of not.

Aiden: Shut the fuck up, both of you.

Cole: What happened?

Aiden: She's spending more time with him than with me.

Xander: That's bad.

Aiden: And she ignores me when he's around.

Ronan: May he rest in peace. That is, if you didn't kill him already.

Aiden: That's the thing. I can't kill him.

Xander: Why not? I'd do it in a heartbeat if anyone took up Kim's time.

Ronan: Who is it? We'll do it for you. Lars learnt how to hide bodies.

Cole: It's Eli.

Xander: WHAT? You're jealous of your own fucking son, King?

Aiden: He takes her time and he's being a little shit about it, making a face at me behind her back.

Cole: I hate him a little less now.

Aiden: Why the hell do you hate him? What's wrong with my son?

Cole: The fact that he's your son. And that he keeps roaming around my Ava like a shadow. I mean it, I'm breaking his legs before he comes near her.

Ronan: I like him, though. If I had a daughter, I'd definitely give her to him. Speaking of which, Xan, you still didn't change your mind about Cecily for Remi?

Xander: Fuck you, Ron. My Cecily won't be anyone's but ours.

Ronan: Your loss, *mon ami.* There's Glyn and Ava and they'll fight over my Rem.

Cole: Leave my daughter out of this or you'll regret it, Ron.

Levi: Submit a proposition with favourable conditions and I might consider giving Glyn away.

Ronan: Now we're talking. Let me tell Remi the news. He should be okay with it since I taught him to keep his options open.

Ronan: Who the fuck stole my stash of weed?

Xander: You had a stash of weed and didn't tell us?

Levi: Why would you think it's one of us?

Ronan: Because it was there last night when we had Dad Day with the kids while the women went shopping. And by the way, I hate Dad Day. I don't like Teal alone out there.

Cole: She wasn't alone, technically.

Aiden: Says the one who was obsessively checking on his wife.

Xander: Says the one who actually took his son and went after his wife.

Levi: Says the one who suggested we all do the same.

Ronan: Bottom line, Dad Day sucks. That's why I needed the weed. We should do something to stop them from going out alone.

Xander: Nah. Green says they need their alone time away from us and the kids.

Ronan: Away from us?

Levi: Us? As in, ALL OF US?

Xander: I know, right? I didn't think Kimmy would ever want time away from me.

Aiden: You're the one everyone needs time away from. And Astor. Nash, too. Levi, sometimes. I'm the only one Elsa doesn't need time away from.

Cole: Is that why she hid when you went to find her?

Aiden: That's because she was trying something on and saving it as a surprise. Speak for yourself. Silver hugged Ava and not you.

Cole: It's the hormones, idiot. She tries to control them in public.

Aiden: Yeah, right.

Xander: *laughing out loud emoji*

Levi: *laughing out loud emoji*

Ronan: *laughing out loud emoji* Now, back to my weed. Who touched it?

Xander: Where did you hide it?

Ronan: Where do you think? Underneath a flower pot. I got the good stuff and hid it from Teal because she doesn't like its smell in the house. I spent a lot on this stash and got it from overseas. It's my weekly break.

Cole: What a shame for it to go down the drain.

Ronan: You fucking…

Xander: Uh-oh.

Cole: Remember when you burnt the book that I spent so much time and effort to get from overseas? Well, payback's a bitch.

Ronan: *Connard!*

Aiden: As I always say and no one believes me, Cole is a petty little bitch.

TWENTY-SEVEN

The Women's Group Chat

Kimberly: Can I say that I'm so glad we decided to have our own group chat? The men aren't the only ones who get that.

Astrid: I had a peek at Levi's phone by accident the other day and all they do is fight over there.

Silver: Cole says he's just there because Ronan usually makes a fool out of himself.

Teal: Cole will have me to speak to.

Silver: Oops.

Elsa: And we even have Aurora with us.

Astrid: But Jonathan isn't with the men in the group chat.

Aurora: Jonathan doesn't do texting. He only uses emails. He's a snob that way.

Silver: Imagine if he were there, though. With both Aiden and Levi.

Kimberly: *shivers emoji*

Astrid: We already get that in family dinners. It's more than enough.

Aurora: Amen to that.

Teal: I think it would be fun.

Elsa: Did you just call that fun?

Teal: Yeah, I mean they're all part of the same family. It's even more fun when Jonathan meets Dad and Agnus.

Elsa: More like chaotic.

Aurora: Nah. It's more than that *winking emoji*

Astrid: What do you mean?

Aurora: Well, now that Jonathan and Ethan are actual friends again, Agnus doesn't seem to like it.

Elsa: Agnus doesn't like anyone.

Teal: Hey! That's not true.

Elsa: Teal, honey, I know Agnus raised you and Knox, but he's still a psycho.

Teal: He is not. He has a heart underneath it all. You just refuse to see it.

Kimberly: Uh-oh. Ron won't be happy if he learns you're defending Agnus.

Teal: You think?

Aurora: Point is, the whole thing between Jonathan, Ethan, and Agnus is a lot more than you girls think. You'll see.

Teal: Ronan was complaining about Dad Day earlier and made Remi hold a sign that says 'Petition to Cancel Dad Day', signed by all the other kids.

Kimberly: Except for Cecily because she likes that day way too much to even think about cancelling it.

Astrid: They'll live.

Elsa: They're just being drama kings. We usually have the kids all the time. They won't die if they have them once a week.

Silver: It's less about the kids and more about us. They dislike that we go out alone.

Kimberly: Cole said that?

Silver: He doesn't have to. I can sense it without him having to say a word. Besides, he was grumbling about it to Papa the other day.

Aurora: Honestly, they will have to suck it.

Astrid: You're one to talk. Jonathan sends his bodyguards after you if you don't answer his calls.

Aurora: But I don't go with them. He's my husband, not my keeper. He'll get used to it, eventually.

Elsa: It's been over ten years, Aurora. I don't think Jonathan will ever get used to it.

Aurora: Well, neither will I.

Kimberly: I feel bad for leaving Xan and Cecily alone, though.

Silver: Stop being a softie, Kim. That's exactly their aim. They want us to feel guilty and cancel the whole thing.

Astrid: Which will not happen, right? I enjoy being husband-and-kid-free.

Teal: We will not bow.

Elsa: Not now. Not ever.

Elsa: Eli asked me today how long it took me to marry his daddy.

Kimberly: Cecily asked where she can find someone like her daddy *laughing emoji*

Astrid: Bran and Lan only ask why the hell we had Glyn. They think she's spoilt and unnecessary. They called their sister unnecessary.

Teal: And then there's Remi, who keeps asking if he came out of me like the cub came from the lioness we watched in the documentary. He had an argument about it with Ronan and didn't speak to him for an hour, thinking his daddy hurt me.

Aurora: He's so cute.

Silver: Ava barely talks and whenever she does, it's to call her daddy's name. I'm scared she'll be jealous once the baby is born.

Kimberly: She'll be fine. I'm pretty sure she will love her baby sister or brother. Besides, do you think Cole will even let her feel jealous?

Astrid: She's right. Eli wasn't jealous of Lan and Bran when they were born.

Aurora: That's because he was already spoilt shitless by all of us.

Elsa: Eli is weird these days. He's always holding on to Aiden and asking him if there's a way to make a pact of marriage.

Teal: What does he even mean by a pact of marriage?

Elsa: No clue, but it seems that my little boy is in a hurry.

Silver: What did Aiden say?

Elsa: What do you think? He supports him every

step of the way and told him he'll even take care of his Uncle Cole if he needs to.

Silver: Uh-oh. I think I know where this is going.

Elsa: Me, too. It won't be pretty.

Teal: But it will be fun.

THE END

Up next is a thrilling arranged mafia romance with explosive characters. *Pre-order Throne of Power* now!

Curious about Aiden's domineering father, Jonathan King? You can read his story in *Reign of a King.*

WHAT'S NEXT?

Thank you so much for reading *Royal Elite Epilogue*! If you liked it, please leave a review.
Your support means the world to me.

If you're thirsty for more discussions with other readers of the series, you can join the Facebook group, *Rina Kent's Spoilers Room*.

If you're looking to what to read next, jump into *Reign of a King* to read about Aiden's father and Levi's uncle, the ruthless Jonathan King.

P.S. Yes, there is a series for the horsemen's children, and it's titled *Legacy of Gods*. You can start with *God of Malice*.

ALSO BY RINA KENT

For more books by the author and a reading
order, please visit:

www.rinakent.com/books

ABOUT THE AUTHOR

Rina Kent is a *USA Today*, international, and #1 Amazon bestselling author of everything enemies to lovers romance.

She's known to write unapologetic anti-heroes and villains because she often fell in love with men no one roots for. Her books are sprinkled with a touch of darkness, a pinch of angst, and an unhealthy dose of intensity.

She spends her private days in London laughing like an evil mastermind about adding mayhem to her expanding universe. When she's not writing, Rina travels, hikes, and spoils cats in a pure Cat Lady fashion.

If you're in the mood to stalk me:

Website: www.rinakent.com

Newsletter: www.subscribepage.com/rinakent

BookBub: www.bookbub.com/profile/rina-kent

Amazon: www.amazon.com/Rina-Kent/e/
B07MM54G22

Goodreads: www.goodreads.com/author/
show/18697906.Rina_Kent

Instagram: www.instagram.com/author_rina

Facebook: www.facebook.com/rinaakent

Reader Group: www.facebook.com/groups/rinakent.
club

Pinterest: www.pinterest.co.uk/AuthorRina/boards

Tiktok: www.tiktok.com/@rina.kent

Twitter: twitter.com/AuthorRina

Made in the USA
Monee, IL
21 March 2024